Ladue

Neal R. Minor

DEDICATION

Thank you Melissa for encouraging me to finish what I started. I just needed a little nudge.

I want to thank each of my friends and family members who reviewed the rough draft and provided much needed feedback. I like to write, but I'm certainly not a grammar and punctuation expert. It was invaluable to the finished product to hear other interpretations of my work. Thank you again; Miranda, JoAnn, Ashley and Linda.

And thank you Miranda for sharing your design talent with me and putting together a captivating book cover.

ACKNOWLEDGMENTS

During my senior year in high school, my English teacher, Mrs. Linda Hays, suggested that I should be a writer. I don't think I laughed out loud at her, but I'm sure I probably rolled my eyes. Back then, I wrote because I had an assignment. Over time, I've continued to write because I enjoy it. I write for me, to get the thoughts out of my head and on the paper. It was only recently that I considered putting those thoughts together in one coherent piece of work that could be considered a book. Unfortunately, there were too many thoughts and too many books with too many different plots going on at one time. Then my wonderful Melissa, my eternal optimist, who honestly believes that I can accomplish anything, asked me to please, finish just one book.

I want all of the teachers who read this; and the coaches, the mentors, the tutors and instructors to know…if you ever wonder if your students are listening, if you ever wonder if you're getting through to them, if you ever want to know if you're making a difference; you are. Maybe not always in the way you want, but they are listening. You are getting through to them and you are making a difference. Keep up the good work.

So, here you go Mrs. Hays. After 23 years, maybe you were right. Maybe I should have been a writer.

DISCLAIMER

This book is a work of fiction. Names, characters, places and incidents are a product of the author's imagination or are used fictitiously. Any resemblance to actual events or locales or persons, living or dead, is entirely coincidental.

INTRODUCTION

Rob Anderson is a man with a plan. From a young age he has had his entire life mapped out. He knows exactly what he's going to do, when he's going to do it and who is going to be by his side. His only problem might be getting everyone else to go along with his plan. When reality doesn't match the world that Rob has created in his head, he has a hard time adjusting to real life.

Minor

I

I set the last box down in my new bedroom and went to the kitchen for a beer. I still couldn't believe I was going to be living here for the next year. Six bedrooms, eight baths, a swimming pool! As I walked across the marble floor in the dining room, I was grinning like a schoolboy. Hell, just a few months ago, I was a schoolboy, and now I was living in a mansion in Ladue, MO that was everything I ever wanted. Of course, it wasn't my mansion and technically, I was only housesitting, but I was still living here.

I had always assumed that someday Erin and I would have a house of our own just like this. It would take a while and we were in no hurry; it would happen when it was supposed to, according to the plan.

The plan, the worthless plan that we had been working on for so long. The plan that I thought we both understood so well. The plan that Erin had to go and ruin. At least living in this luxury for a while would give me a little taste of what our future would hold and help lessen the sting of Erin's decision not to come with me to St. Louis.

I had graduated in May from the University of Missouri in Columbia, MO. I really wasn't ready for it to be my final semester, but if she and I were going to do things right and follow our plan, I needed to work while she finished law school, and then I would go back to grad school when she was done. What I didn't see coming was her decision to turn down the offer from Washington University to go to law school in Columbia.

It had been our plan all along, but in the end, her reasoning was pretty logical. If I wanted to get ahead at work, I would need to show them how dedicated I was and that would mean working late. Erin would be spending most of her evenings studying. With both of us living in St. Louis, the most we would do is get in each other's way and be a distraction.

If I had known sooner that Erin wasn't coming to St. Louis with me, I might have applied at other places. In the end, St. Louis was the only city I considered and the job at Edward Jones was the best opportunity available here. I had to apply for jobs in St. Louis because of Wash U, where *she* was going to school...it was all part of the plan! But, I guess by being here, she's only two hours away in Columbia and we'll see each other every weekend. And, the reality is, even if we both lived in the same place right now, we would really only see each other on weekends.

Even after it was decided that she would stay in Columbia for law school, I was fully prepared to rent my dream. A loft apartment in the city all by myself. Erin and I used to talk about it in high school; how cool it would be to have a contemporary, loft apartment in the city. Heck, we might not even need a car. It was all part of the plan.

****

Our plan started eight years ago in Shelbyville, MO when we started dating our freshman year in high school. My family has lived in the Shelbyville area for generations. My dad is a farmer, like my grandfather before him and his father before that. We have what's called a Century Farm, because it's been in the same family for over 100 years.

Shelbyville is a typical Midwestern town of just over 500 people. If it wasn't the county seat it probably would have fewer than that. The county is the largest employer, followed by the school district. It's not exactly a booming economy. In addition to the public employers in town there's a convenience store, coffee shop and a farm supply store. It seems that most everyone else is self-employed as a farmer or a contractor.

Shelbyville was a safe, comfortable place to grow up. The same people sit at the same table at the coffee shop every morning. The same families sit in the same pews at church every Sunday. The same festivals and parades take place on the same weekends every year. Planting season and harvest season are used to measure time and the success or failure of those two seasons is directly related to the mood of the community.

Erin's family moved to town the summer before we started high school, when her dad replaced the retiring minister of the Christian Church. Shelbyville isn't the kind of town that sees new families move in very often, so it created quite the buzz among the teens and pre-teens when we learned that a new family, with a daughter entering 9th grade and a son going into 6th had just moved to town.

The boys my age were so stupid and immature about the whole thing. There was a park across the street from the church and the parsonage house and they would sit under the pavilion all day just waiting for her to come outside. As soon as they thought she was looking, they would run to the basketball court to show off their "skills". The whole thing was ridiculous, but I guess that's the way most young teenage boys act around girls.

Not me. I never was into strutting my tail feathers, thumping my chest and showing off. I knew right away that Erin was very cerebral and that kind of crap wasn't going to make an impact on her anyway. She would sit on her front porch, reading a book and mostly ignoring what was going on at the park. Occasionally she might glance over the top of her book to see what kind of nonsense was occurring in the park, but I could tell she wasn't impressed. I had a much better plan to get her attention. Hell, I always had a plan!

We were members of the same church so I just casually mentioned to my mom that we should have a BBQ for the new minister and his family. Mom agreed, although she decided to have it in the park, with the whole congregation, rather than at our house, with just the two families as I had suggested. In the end, it worked out better that way. Erin got to meet me and quite a few of the kids from school and I could tell immediately that I was right about her.

I did more listening than talking during that first meeting. I let the other guys show what asses they were and I just watched and listened, waiting for the right opportunity.

Her father and mother had both grown up in small towns in Iowa. They met in college, with her mother getting a degree in accounting and her father, a degree in business. I guess that after a few years of working for Wells Fargo in Des Moines, he just really wasn't satisfied with the business world and felt the calling to attend the Theological Seminary and minister to those in the inner city.

Both of her parents had felt like small town life somehow left them with fewer opportunities and they decided early on that they needed to live in a bigger place in order to expose their children to more culture.

Fortunately, for Erin and me, after several years of living in Chicago, her parents realized that bigger was definitely not better. While her father's ministry was certainly noble, there was no way they could raise kids in the same neighborhood where they had first lived in the city; a tiny house in an extremely blighted neighborhood, next door to the church.

When Erin started school they moved to a suburb and spent hours of their lives each week in the car; and crime in the city certainly wasn't getting any better. Her parents didn't make enough money to send them to a private school in Chicago and Erin's father didn't want her going to the public high school. Soon enough, he felt that his ministry in the city was complete and it just so happened that Pastor Hollingsworth was retiring from our small town church after 40 years of service.

From that very first meeting, at a church BBQ in the park in Shelbyville, MO at 14 years old, I knew that Erin was the one I would spend the rest of my life with. She just fit perfectly into my plan. She was smart and polite. Even coming from a big city she knew to say "Yes, Sir" and "No, Ma'am." Her favorite class was math, followed by English, just like me. She asked about whether our school had an FBLA club. That was one of the things she was looking forward to about going to high school.

Of course, Steve, being the meathead that he is, replied, "I don't know what a FBLA is, but we have a pretty awesome FFA and I'm going to take you to barn-warming. I'll even pick you up on my Allis-Chalmers tractor. It's a 1937 Model B that me and my dad completely restored."

Good God, he sounded like such a redneck! I was beginning to feel embarrassed, not just for him, but for our whole community! He was still rambling on about horsepower and torque and bon fires and muddin' and I knew I had to say something to rescue her from his ignorance.

"I've always thought that we should have an FBLA club in our school. Not everyone is preparing for life on the farm, I said, glaring at Steve.

"If we get enough people interested I'm sure we can get one started. And if the school won't support it as an official organization, then we can just have an informal club."

"That sounds like a good plan, said Erin.

"I have a lot of ideas that I think could prepare us for FBLA competitions. An FBLA is a Future Business Leaders of America club. Kind of like FFA, but for kids interested in business. They have competitions just like FFA," she said, spelling it out for Steve's ignorant sake.

That was music to my ears. Erin and I spending hours together, building the first ever FBLA club at North Shelby high school. *Of course,* we were meant to be together. I've always been pretty logical and reasonable; wise beyond my years as some in town would say. But, as far as Erin and I meeting and coming together like we did? Well, there had to be a higher power involved. It was just too perfect to have happened by chance.

For the next hour or so, the kids from school peppered her with questions about the big city and what kids do for fun in Chicago. Then they would tell her all about what kids in Shelby County do for fun and all the events of the coming school year that she just couldn't miss. It turns out that Erin really wasn't the displaced city girl that most had expected her to be. Her family lived in a suburb of Chicago and except for church on Sundays, they really didn't go into the city that much. Her junior high classes were pretty much like ours; just in a bigger, newer, shinier building with a few more elective choices and a lot more students.

Since both of her parents had grown up in small towns in Iowa, only about 45 minutes apart, she had spent plenty of time visiting her grandparents' small towns. Shelbyville really wasn't a foreign land to her. She was familiar with 4th of July parades and cafes and tractors on Main Street.

As I watched and listened to her talk, it was mesmerizing. I so wanted to be having a private conversation with her. Just the two of us; maybe sitting in the hayloft of our barn or on the dock of our lake. Just somewhere alone, where the two of us could start planning our life together.

As the kids from school went on about the homecoming bon fire and the annual Shrimp Boil as if they were life-altering cultural events, I made sure to take a picture in my mind. I wanted to remember exactly what Erin looked like the first time we met. She had her wavy, brown hair pulled back into a low ponytail at her neck. Her bangs were pulled over to the left side and she had a thin, stretchy, gold headband worn at the top of her forehead, kind of like a hippie or a flapper girl from the 1920s, to keep the hair out of her eyes. She wore a tight-fitting, red tank top layered with a looser fitting, black tank top and white shorts. A pair of gold sandals that matched the headband completed her attire.

Here it is, eight years later, and I can still remember exactly what she wore the first day we met. I've asked her several times what her first thought was of me. I didn't really expect her to remember exactly what I was wearing, but I thought I would be more of a memory than "quiet and kind of shy."

I was going for sophisticated and intelligent, and I thought that with all the guys from school in their seed-corn hats, sleeveless t-shirts, dirty jeans and roper boots, I might have made a little more of an impression. I guess it was all a little over-whelming for her during that first meeting. There were just too many new people to meet, and I'm sure their ridiculous stories had her head swimming.

Soon the sun was setting and I heard Erin's mom call to her that the mosquitoes were getting bad and they were heading home.

"It was so nice to meet all of you," she said as she started across the street to go home.

"I can't wait for the school year to start."

I was getting ready to tell her it was nice to meet her too and remind her that we could start talking about the FBLA club whenever she was ready when Steve blurted out,

"Don't forget. I'm picking you up on my Allis-Chalmers to go to barn-warming."

"Sure thing. It's a date." She replied.

Oh good Lord! I couldn't believe it. Steve was such an asshole to put her on the spot like that. What was she supposed to do? Be rude? I knew that wasn't her style. At least Steve's attention span is about equal to his IQ, so he was bound to forget by the time barn warming rolled around. I'm sure she was counting on that too.

I walked over to where the church women were cleaning up the food. The men were carrying tables and chairs back to the church basement, and I grabbed a few chairs and headed that way. The churchyard and the yard of her house bordered each other. Maybe Erin would be on the back porch of her house and I could chat for a few more minutes after putting the chairs away.

No such luck, so I walked back over to the park and told my mom I was going to walk home.

"Are you sure Robbie? The mosquitoes are bad and it's almost two miles."

"I know where I live mom, and quit calling me Robbie!"

God I hated being called Robbie. I had outgrown it several years earlier, but hadn't been able to get some people, especially my mom to call me Rob. I never understood how my parents, my teachers and members of the church could say in one breath that I seem very mature and knowledgeable for my age, but still call me Robbie. I may have only been 14 years old, but my brain was developed beyond my years.

It had always been difficult to relate to kids my own age. Mainly because the other teenagers in Shelbyville thought that life started and ended with high school sports and bonfires. I know the reason I didn't have a lot of friends and it was hard to relate was because I was on a different cognitive level than them. Thank God Erin moved to town when she did.

That night I walked north along County Road 249, hoping the entire way that my parents had taken the highway. My mom knew I would walk the gravel and the last thing I wanted was for my parents and little brother pulling up beside me and trying to get me to get in the truck. Fate was on my side and I didn't see a vehicle the whole way home. By the time I got to the front porch, I had pretty much planned the life that Erin and I would spend together.

II

I walked downstairs to the amazing rec room, which was all mine - for the next twelve months anyway. I opened the beer, sat down on the couch and turned on Sports Center on the 110-inch flat screen.

I had stopped at Best Buy in St. Charles on my way in to Ladue today to get a new charger for my phone. My Uncle Rich had told me about how big the TV was at this house, so I had to see for myself at Best Buy how much it cost.

$39,000!!!!

I was watching Sports Center on a TV that cost more than I was making at my first job! Of course, it would be so much better if Erin were sitting here with me. We wouldn't be able to watch Sports Center if she were here; she would want to watch HGTV or something like that, but at least she would be sitting with me.

I snapped a picture of the TV with my phone and texted it to her.

"Can you imagine watching The Walking Dead on this?"

Five minutes, no reply. Ten minutes, no reply. Twenty minutes, no reply! What in the hell could she be doing? She can't even try to tell me that she's studying. Classes don't start for two more weeks!

"Come on Rob; be logical, not emotional" I told myself. "I'm sure she has a very good reason for not replying right away. Maybe her parents are in town and they went out for lunch."

Although, I think that she would tell me if her parents decided to come to town. I really wanted her to come with me this weekend to help me get moved in and see the house, but she claimed to have too much to do to get herself ready for school.

The beer was good, but I was going to have to try out one of Ambassador Nichols' single malt scotches' from the bar. I had never even had scotch, but if I was going to be living in a mansion in Ladue, I should probably learn to drink what my peers drink. There were about 40 different bottles that said scotch on the label. I had no idea which one to try. I finally found a bottle with a label I couldn't pronounce and poured myself a glass of Tomintoul 27 year old scotch.

It burned on the way down, but I think I could get used to it. I remember my Uncle Rich talking about all these expensive bottles of scotch from the Christmas party he went to here. It was just about eight months ago when we were all home in Shelbyville for Christmas that Uncle Rich first brought up the idea of us house-sitting.

My Uncle Rich had left the farm and gone away to college, never to return to small town life. One of his fraternity brothers was a guy named Brian Nichols, whose dad owned an electric motor company in St. Louis. Uncle Rich was always a smooth talker and just had a way with meeting new people. He always fit right in and made people feel comfortable.

****

During their freshman year of college, Uncle Rich had gone to Brian's house in St. Louis for the weekend. Brian's parents were having a party and they and their guests were pretty impressed with this down-home, small-town kid and his ability to converse in any situation.

Brian was getting his degree in mechanical engineering with a plan to go home and take over the family business; building bigger, better, more efficient electric motors. Over the years, Uncle Rich spent quite a bit of time with Brian and his family. Brian was an only child and the Nichols's made sure to include Uncle Rich in tailgates at Mizzou football games, family trips and even the occasional holiday gathering.

Uncle Rich was also a bit of a math geek and when he left North Shelby High School, he had planned to return and be the high school math teacher. It seemed like a safe, comfortable job and for a kid from the farm; there was nothing wrong with that.

However, after spending some time with Brian's family and seeing what was really available in the world outside Shelby County, Uncle Rich knew he would never come back. There was money to be made all over this world, just not in Shelbyville. By the time he graduated, he had a degree in economics and was planning to go to graduate school and get an MBA.

One weekend, when Brian's parents were in town, they took Brian and Uncle Rich out to dinner at The Heidelberg; where Uncle Rich had just given up his bartending job in anticipation of graduating and starting on his MBA. I'd heard the story so many times I could tell it like it was my own.

"Rich, are you excited about starting grad school?" asked Mr. Nichols.

"Yes sir, I am."

"Any idea what your area of focus is going to be?"

"I'm leaning toward finance. It seems like that's where the money is and my plan is do everything I can to make money."

"Uh huh. Well there's money to be made, that's for sure. You know those hedge fund managers? The guys who make $10, $20 million a year? You could be one of those guys Rich."

"That's the plan Mr. Nichols."

"But what kind of life would you really have? You'd have more money than you ever dreamed of, but you'd be working 100 hours a week. Do you ever plan on getting married? Having kids? Having any sort of life outside of work?"

"Well sure. I just figure I can put in the 100 hours a week for a few years until I have a nest egg built up. Then I can cut back on my hours and try to find a bride. By the time I have kids; I'll still be able to make good money and only have to put in about 50-60 hours a week, like most people do anyway."

"Uh huh. Well it sounds like you have it all planned out Rich. When you're done with grad school, if you ever need an introduction or a reference, you just let me know."

"Thank you Mr. Nichols, I really appreciate it."

"You know, Rich have you ever thought about sales? Brian and I have been talking about some of his ideas. He's going to start immediately on a new product line that he's been working on the past few years. It's going to revolutionize the market place in the same way that the assembly line did. The thing is; the best product in the world isn't any good to anyone if they don't know about it.

"I haven't hired a new sales rep in 20 years. I started out doing my own selling until the company grew too big. Then when it was time to hire sales people, I hired guys that I liked talking with. I could teach anyone to talk about the product, but I needed guys that could talk about the weather and the ball game and relate to the customer.

"The first salesman I hired was a guy that I golfed with. He had been a UPS driver before I hired him, but he could talk. He could talk to anyone about anything at any time. He just retired last year. He has a vacation cabin outside Jackson, Wyoming.

"You see Rich, sales is king! And it doesn't take an MBA to be a great salesman. It takes someone who is ambitious and can talk. Rich, no matter what you do, you're going to be successful, it's just who you are, because people like you. They can trust you. If you want to sit in a cubicle and crunch numbers all day and make millions of dollars, then Brian will probably come calling when he needs some capital to expand a product line. But, if you want to travel the world, meet interesting people, attend the World Series with clients and utilize your gift of gab to make your millions, well, we could certainly use someone like you."

And, as they say, the rest is history.

Brian and Uncle Rich moved to St. Louis and got an apartment together. Uncle Rich learned about the products and Mr. Nichols sent him out to sell. With Brian's patented, redesigned motors, they practically sold themselves. Before long people were calling Uncle Rich to see if he could come meet with them. He found a niche selling to the oil extraction industry and spent some time traveling to the Persian Gulf and the Gulf of Mexico.

It was on one of his sales trips to Baton Rouge, LA that he met his future wife, Shelby. Shelby was a student at LSU and was waiting tables at a little steakhouse where Uncle Rich was meeting with a client. Apparently, she turned him down flat when he asked her what time her shift ended, but after several more trips to Baton Rouge over the next few months he won her over.

He also moved to Baton Rouge, where he still lives today. Uncle Rich continued working for Brian, even after Brian moved the manufacturing plant to Lima, Peru in the mid 80s. It was this move to Peru that made Brian's company a global leader in electric motors and the reason why, after his retirement, the Peruvian Government petitioned the US Government to appoint him ambassador.

When Uncle Rich and Aunt Shelby were on their way to Shelbyville last December for Christmas, which would end up being the last one with Grandma Katherine, they stopped in St. Louis for a Christmas party at Brian's house in Ladue.

Brian was talking to Uncle Rich about his ambassadorship and asked if Rich's oldest daughter would be interested in house sitting for a year. Rich's oldest daughter Adeline was a sophomore at LSU and really wouldn't be able to take a year off and live in St. Louis, but Uncle Rich mentioned me, his nephew, who was about ready to graduate in May and was applying for jobs in St. Louis. Brian told him to mention it to me, which he did at Christmas, and if I ended up in St. Louis, then the house was mine.

Of course, my first call was to Erin. I knew that she was at her Grandparent's house in Iowa that evening and that her whole family was there, but I had to tell her. Maybe it would change her mind about Wash U.

III

A few days after fall semester finals of our senior year, Erin and I had gone out to eat dinner. It had become our ritual since our first semester at MU. Finals would get over and before we headed home for the break, we would go out for dinner. Our first semester we were both so broke that I had to sell back my textbooks just to be able to take her to SubWay.

This year however, I had been saving back a little money from each paycheck. My job as a policy analyst at Shelter Insurance sucked, but I needed some sort of real-life, professional experience on my resume if I was going to be applying for real-life, professional jobs. Apparently, according to my college advisor, delivery driver for Jimmy Johns and sales associate at Best Buy didn't adequately prepare me for the world of high finance.

I really didn't think that the job at Shelter required much more brain power than any other job I'd had, but I guess I was supposed to work in a shirt and tie environment prior to applying for real jobs. As much as the job sucked, it did pay much better than I was used to making and I was going to treat Erin to a fabulous dinner. After all, we would only get to do this one more time before our tradition ended with graduation. Then we'd have to start a new tradition together.

We were at Sophia's, an upscale Italian-Mediterranean restaurant on the South side of town. I asked Erin what sounded good for an appetizer and she mentioned the Sun-Dried Tomato Hummus Plate. It was the cheapest appetizer on the menu!

"We can get whatever you want Erin. I've been saving up for this dinner for three months. Anything on the menu. Whatever you want. I've got it covered."

"Rob, I really like the hummus plate here."

"You've been here? When did you come here to eat?"

"Rob, we've lived in Columbia for four years. I've been here several times, usually with my sorority sisters."

Of course, the sorority sisters. The snobby brats with Daddy's credit card. God, I hated her sorority sisters and I have no idea why I ever let her join a sorority.

Our freshman year Erin even tried talking me into joining a fraternity. I know that's how Uncle Rich met Brian and if it hadn't been for the fraternity, he'd be teaching math at North Shelby High School. I went to one Greek party with her our first week on campus. It was just like back home, but the guys traded in their cut up t-shirts, dirty jeans and ropers for polo shirts, douche-bag golf shorts and Sperry's. It wasn't my thing.

Erin and I had a plan, and it didn't include Greek organizations. As long as we stuck to the plan, we wouldn't need the help of our rich friend's parents to help us get jobs. We were there to study and graduate, get jobs, and stick to the plan.

Since she was in a sorority house and I wanted nothing to do with a fraternity, I lived in the dorms until my senior year when I got an apartment with Bimal, whom I had met working at Best Buy.

All throughout college, Erin was always busy with her sorority sisters doing "Greek stuff". She tried to explain to me one time that while she *was* in college to study and graduate and get a job, that she was also there to make new friends and have new experiences.

Whatever!

I decided not to protest too much. This really was her last opportunity to be a kid, and in all of our years together, it was the only major disagreement we had had. I knew she would be serious about her studies and when she went to Wash U, like we always talked about, she would leave her silly sorority behind.

This brings me back to our dinner conversation at Sophia's, where, apparently Erin had eaten before. When Erin joined a sorority, that was the first time she threw a wrench in our plans, but it was nothing compared to the bomb she was about to drop.

"So, Rob, where all have you applied this week?" she said as she placed a dainty spoonful of hummus on a dainty looking cracker.

"A couple more places in St. Louis. Enterprise, Edward Jones, BJC and KPMG." I said, wishing I had just ordered for us. The raw Ahi tuna flatbread was the most expensive appetizer on the menu! That was the one I wanted! Not this vegan, hippie, organic crap on a cracker. She had definitely been in that Sorority too long.

She was nodding her head and asking another question, but I was looking at the menu. I was going to fix this situation by ordering both of our entrees. And I was going to order the Brandy Cream Filet, the most expensive thing on the menu!

"Rob?

"Rob, do any of them sound like promising leads?"

"Yes, actually I already got a reply back from Edward Jones. They're holding a career fair the same week as our Spring Break. They asked that I come to that and I can meet with the hiring managers from several different departments at one time."

"That's awesome. So, it sounds like St. Louis is where you want to be?"

"Hasn't that been the plan all along Erin?"

"Oh, I know that's what you've always talked about. It's just that when it comes time for a career, you have to go where your best option is. You can't limit yourself geographically and miss out on a great opportunity somewhere else."

I didn't even know what the hell she was talking about. Limit myself geographically?

We had our whole lives mapped out; we would go to MU and I would get a degree in finance and she in political science. We both had full ride academic scholarships and we would graduate debt free.

Then we would move to St. Louis and live in a really cool, one bedroom, loft apartment in Lafayette Square. My job would help pay part of her tuition at Washington University School of Law and when she finished school it would be my turn to go back. We knew what kind of jobs we were going to have, when we would buy our first house, have our first child, buy a bigger house, have another child, etc.

Eventually, our life would be complete when we lived in a mansion with a three-car garage and a pool and really cool rec room in the basement with a 110-inch flat screen TV, with grown kids and grandkids running around in the yard after Thanksgiving dinner.

She must have noticed the disgust on my face.

"Rob? Is something wrong? You don't look too good."

Thankfully, our server arrived at the table to take our order. I felt like I didn't even know the person I was talking to.

"Have you decided on an entrée?"

"Yes." I answered, "We'll both have the Brandy Crème Filet, medium rare."

"Actually, I was going to order the Spinach Salad with grilled salmon," stated Erin.

"That's not really what you want is it?"

"Yes, Rob. That *is* what I really want. I can order for myself."

I had never seen her like this. It's as if these sorority girls were messing with her head.

"I guess she wants a salad tonight. At least it's a cheap date for me!

"Can I order us some wine? Or do you want a glass of water with lemon?"

"A glass of chardonnay would be great Rob. Thank you."

"We'll take a bottle of the Cakebread Cellars Chardonnay." I told the server.

"Rob, that's an $80 bottle of wine. The house chardonnay would have been fine," Erin stated as the server walked away.

"Erin, I told you, I've been saving up for this dinner. I want to splurge."

"Ok, but you didn't need to order a bottle. I don't know if I'm going to have more than one glass."

I'm sure if she had been back at the sorority house with the girls she would be downing glass after glass of cheap Yellow Tail or Barefoot, but she couldn't enjoy a night out with me? So what if we were a little tipsy when we left! We were one semester away from completing the next step of the plan.

"Rob, as I was saying before. This is your career and you shouldn't limit yourself geographically. Right now, you're young and you don't have any responsibilities or anything to tie you down. You should explore all of your options and go wherever the best opportunity is."

No responsibility? Nothing to tie me down? How about being tied to the plans that we have? How about the responsibility of being the one that makes sure we follow through with the plan?!

Apparently seven years of planning means nothing to this girl. We have a plan and I'm following through with my end of the bargain. Next, she's going to tell me that she's not going to Wash U!

"Erin, I'm not sure why you're talking about going somewhere other than St. Louis. Are you trying to tell me that you're not going to Wash U?"

"Actually, I've applied to several law schools. I'm not sure where I'm going yet, but I'm really leaning toward staying here in Columbia."

If she thought I didn't look well before, I don't know what she thought now. If my face looked how I felt she would have called an ambulance. My head started swimming and I saw black spots in front of my eyes. I felt a strange tingle in my chest and I could feel my face go flush and the perspiration soak my shirt collar. There was a sharp ringing in my ears. I tried to say something – anything - but my mouth was dry.

Thankfully, our wine arrived. I think the server poured me a taste and asked if it was okay, but I just downed it in one swallow and pointed to the glass.

After the server had filled both of the glasses and left the table, I guess Erin finally sensed that I had an issue with her staying in Columbia.

"Rob, are you sure you're okay?"

I don't really remember much after that. Our food came, and I ate a little bit of it and asked for a box for the rest. I did, however finish my $80 bottle of wine while she was talking about the cost of school and getting to know several of the law professors at MU through her part time job and some opportunity in Jefferson City when she graduates.

This was definitely not part of the plan. I can't believe she just made these decisions without discussing them with me. There had to be someone in that sorority influencing her because we used to discuss everything. She used to tell me all of her ideas, and they all fit perfectly into the plan. Now she was ruining it all!

By the time I paid the bill all I could think about was what a waste of money it was, and the fact that I didn't care if Bimal ate the leftovers in the fridge while I was home visiting my family for Christmas.

IV

It was time to try another taste from Ambassador Nichols' famous scotch collection. This time I choose something I could pronounce, a Glenfiddich 50 year old. I looked out the doors toward the pool. It just *looked* hot outside, but mid-afternoon in late August in Missouri usually is. I decided that when the sun went down and the Cardinal's game started it would probably be cool enough to sit outside. In fact, I was thinking that I could probably sit in the pool and be able to see the game on TV inside once it got dark.

It was a Saturday afternoon. Monday would be Labor Day, and I didn't have to start my new job until Tuesday. My girlfriend was two hours away and wouldn't answer my text messages because she was too busy getting ready to start law school or some bullshit crap like that. My parents encouraged me to leave Shelbyville early this morning and get my stuff moved in so I could become acquainted with the area and the commute to my office over the weekend. I didn't know a single soul in town or have anything to do for three days. I decided that I was going to get drunk, on Ambassador Nichols' dime.

When I arrived here today, just before noon, I used the key pad on the garage to get in. Ambassador Nichols had reprogrammed it to my birthday, 06/23, so I wouldn't forget. I pulled my 1998 Toyota Camry into a garage that was bigger, and cleaner than my parent's house back in Shelbyville. I entered the house into a laundry room and there on the counter was a house key, a garage door opener and an envelope.

The envelope had a letter from Ambassador Nichols thanking me for housesitting for him. He had a few instructions about how the thermostat worked, when the maid and the pest control people and lawn care and pool guy would come by. He left the phone numbers of a few people in the neighborhood if I needed anything and said he would send me an email from his office in Peru once he was settled in so I would have his current contact information. He also explained that the Second Master suite on the west end of the first floor was mine and that I should make myself at home here for the next year. He also included a $100 bill and told me to go somewhere nice for dinner; he suggested Molly's in Soulard.

I had planned on getting acquainted with the whole house and four acres of perfectly manicured property, but by the time I carried in my boxes and clothes, I was ready for a beer and forgot to look around.

I took my scotch, went back to the main floor, and then up the winding staircase to the second floor. There was a sitting lounge at the top of the landing and four bedrooms, each with a walk-in closet and its own bathroom. It was pretty standard mansion stuff. Another door lead to a large closet full of extra linens and a stacked washer/dryer unit. Apparently, it would be too much work to carry laundry downstairs to wash.

Next to that was a door that went to an attic, but it wasn't quite like our attic back home. The Ambassador used it for storage, but with a little paint and some carpet, it would have been just as finished as the rest of the house. I walked over to a bay window in the attic and could see the street that I came in on. I went to the window on the back of the house and could see the entire back yard. I could even see into the neighbor's back yard on the east side of the house and part of a golf course to the southwest. I made a mental note to check out the guesthouse by the pool and the gardening shed when I went outside.

Back down on the first floor was the kitchen and dining room that I had already seen and the hallway leading to my suite. The front of the house had a formal living room and some sort of sitting room with a piano. Off the other end of the kitchen was another hallway with two locked doors.   I assumed that was probably the Ambassador's master suite and maybe an office or something.

I walked out the front door and around the corner of the house. I peered in the windows of the rooms that were locked and sure enough, one was a wood paneled office/library and the other was a huge master suite. By the time I got around to the back yard, I was drenched in sweat. Exploring the backyard would have to wait because the humidity was unbearable. It reminded me of my first and only trip to the State of Louisiana.

****

I remember that the first time Erin and I met, at the barbeque in the park, prior to the start of our freshman year of high school, it was a Friday night. My family was leaving on vacation the next day to go visit my Uncle Rich and Aunt Shelby in Baton Rouge. We had never been on a family vacation outside the state of Missouri and I had been looking forward to it all summer. Now that I had met Erin, I really didn't want to leave her for two weeks. As I packed my bag I was imagining the damage the kids from school, especially Steve, might do while I was gone.

There was nothing I could do about it. At 7:00 am the next morning, we piled in the Tahoe and headed south. I really was excited to see somewhere new, visit Uncle Rich, and see his house. Uncle Rich was my inspiration to get a degree in finance and an MBA.

I loved my dad and thought very highly of his work ethic and the way he took care of our family, but there was no way that I was coming back to the farm. I'm just glad I had heard Uncle Rich's stories enough when I was a kid to know ahead of time that I was getting out of here and not coming back.

I know that Uncle Rich made his money in sales, but that really wasn't for me. I had plenty of self-confidence, I just never felt the need to interact with complete strangers like he could, and I certainly didn't have his 'gift of gab'. However, his original idea of the world of high finance was something I could do. I loved math, I loved numbers and I had no problem sitting in a cubicle crunching numbers while I made my fortune.

It was a long, twelve-hour drive and I was still two years away from getting my first cell phone. My brother was watching movies the whole way and I was daydreaming about Erin. I went over in my head what I had planned while walking home the night before, and what I had refined while laying awake most of the night.

I already knew that she liked me; just by the way we connected at the barbeque. She was probably home doing the same thing I was, planning our future together. As soon as we got back from our vacation, I was going to go to her house and ask if she wanted to discuss her ideas for the FBLA club. That would lead to hours of discussion between just the two of us.

I would probably invite her to the farm to go fishing or just hiking through the woods. My parents would probably invite her family over for dinner once or twice before the summer was over and by the time school started, everyone would know that we were dating.

I had most of the details worked out; where we would walk, the things that I would say and how she would reply. I was still a little fuzzy about when I would first try to hold her hand, but I had it narrowed down to two or three different moments within the next six weeks; most likely it would be while we were sitting on the dock fishing as the sun set over the lake. I was pretty sure that would be the moment.

I didn't have plans for every single day of high school because I wanted to remain flexible in case Erin came up with a good idea of something we could do together, but I had thought quite a bit about what we would both wear to each of the homecoming dances and to prom. Since homecoming happened before barn warming and everyone would know we were dating by then, there was no way she was going to barn warming with Steve. He'd just have to get over it.

I always knew we would have a daughter named Katherine, but we'd call her Katy for short. It was a family name on both my mother and father's side. As we drove through Memphis on the way to Baton Rouge, I was still trying to decide what Erin and I would name our son. Looking out the window I saw a sign for Sam Cooper Blvd and decided right then that we would name our son Cooper.

I'd like to say that I really enjoyed the trip that summer, but my main focus was thinking about my life with Erin. Uncle Rich's daughters were quite a bit younger than me and they and my brother spent most of the trip in the swimming pool. It was amazingly hot and humid in southern Louisiana and I thought about swimming, but what I really wanted to do was discuss my school and career plans with Uncle Rich. However, I don't think that he was taking me as serious as I was. It had been two years since we had seen Uncle Rich and I'm pretty sure he still thought of me as his silly little nephew. The reality was that I had matured a lot in two years and was very wise beyond my 14 years. I already had a plan for my entire life, including a wife and a career in high finance.

Finally, on the day that we all went to New Orleans, the girls rode with Mom and Aunt Shelby in one car and the guys rode in the other. I had a chance to discuss my financial future with Uncle Rich. He gave me a lot of good advice about what I can do now to prepare for college and the classes I needed to take once I got to college. He said it was important to have a 'real' job or internship while in college and he mentioned that I shouldn't limit myself geographically when I graduate and look for my first job.

I know he was just trying to be helpful and didn't know about my plans with Erin, but it was already decided that we were both going to St. Louis after college. He also mentioned that I shouldn't be so focused on finance because I could miss other opportunities that might come along. He said something about life being full of surprises, some good and some bad, but that's what makes life so enjoyable.

Uncle Rich was fun to talk to and he was usually a jokester. He always made people feel comfortable and laugh. However, he wasn't very good at the philosophical stuff; so when he said that knowing the destination before the journey even starts is like reading the last chapter of a book first - it takes all the mystery and excitement out of it. I knew that he just didn't understand the significance of my plan.

Uncle Rich kept asking me all kinds of questions about what sports I was going to play in high school, as if that had anything to do with preparing me for a career in high finance. I certainly wasn't going to play football or basketball with those meatheads from school.

I had found out in junior high that I could run really far and not get tired. Running was something I enjoyed doing and I was good at it, so track was the only sport that I planned to participate in. Erin hadn't mentioned anything about athletics at the barbeque, but she was in really good shape. I'm sure she was a runner too.

The day in New Orleans was probably my favorite of the whole trip. I imagined everything that Erin and I would do if we were there on vacation together. I made a mental note that we should plan a spring break trip to the French Quarter during our junior year of college.

Finally, we were heading back to Missouri. The trip home seemed to take forever. The whole trip for me was spent thinking about Erin and the conversations we would have and things we would do once I got back. It was getting dark when we passed the Arch in St. Louis and we still had almost three hours to go. I wasn't going to be able to talk to Erin when we got home that night, but first thing the next day I was going to take her the Mardi Gras mask and beads that I had got for her in New Orleans. The beads were red and yellow, just like our school colors and she would probably wear them to all of the football and basketball games.

V

It was time for another scotch. I chose another one I couldn't pronounce, Laphroaig Triple Wood 18 year. I tried to call Erin and it went straight to her voicemail. What in the hell could she be doing? It had been three hours since I sent her that text and she still hadn't replied. I didn't know whether to be pissed or worried.

I had found the movie *Fight Club* on TV and was settled in to the recliner for the next few hours until it got dark and cooled off outside. I turned up the volume to test out the surround sound so I'm not sure when the noise from the neighbor's house started, but when the movie got quiet I could definitely hear some head-banger music coming from close by.

I looked out the French doors, but from the basement, I could only see my backyard. I went upstairs and looked out the kitchen window, but still couldn't see over to the neighbors. I was sure the sound wasn't coming from the golf course. I went all the way up to the attic and looked out the south window toward the neighbor on the east. There in the driveway was a black, 1970s muscle car and some guy working under the hood.

I watched him for a good 10 minutes, occasionally glancing toward the golf course. After watching a group tee off on the course I looked back toward the guy working on the car. There was a girl in skimpy shorts and a tank top bringing him a beer. It was so hot outside. Why in the world would he be working on his car right now?

Ladue

I wondered who he was. Maybe the homeowner's son or grandson? And the chick in the skimpy shorts? Probably his flavor of the week. I started making up a story in my head about who he could be. He looked like he might be in his mid to late 20s. He was wearing those stupid jeans with large, embroidered crosses on the pockets and a t-shirt and Nike shoes. Nothing about him looked like he was the son or grandson of a wealthy family. He looked like most of the douche-bags from back home or from the fraternities at college.

He probably doesn't have any sort of real job and just sponges off his rich family. He was probably given the car for his sixteenth birthday and he works on it all the time because they won't buy him another car and he has to keep it running. Although he doesn't work a job, apparently, he has plenty of time to work out at the gym and he wears *TapOut* t-shirts that are too small in order to show off his biceps and pecs. I'm also pretty sure he uses part of his allowance on steroids.

The bimbo? He probably just met her at a club last night and is trying to impress her by hanging out at his parent's house while they're out of town. She'll probably be long gone and move on to the next douche-bag as soon as she realizes the truth.

Yep, I had these two completely figured out. I had a fairly smug grin on my face as I thought about how much better Erin and I were than this pair. I glanced once more toward the golf course and then back to the driveway; and they were both staring back at me. I raised my glass of scotch in their direction and the guy gave me a head nod before getting back to work on his car.

As I walked back down to the basement to finish my movie I was thinking about how perfect Erin and I really were together. It was so refreshing to go through high school and college without playing the silly dating games that other people our age played. Never in my life did I have to drag some bimbo home from a club and risk waking up with an STD.

Actually, Erin and I were saving ourselves for marriage. We felt very strongly about consummating our relationship for the first time *on* our wedding night. In fact, we didn't really even do a lot of making out. It just wasn't our style. We felt that that was something too that should wait for marriage. We had kissed once, back in high school. It was a little awkward and I knew immediately that even though we were in a committed relationship, Erin really wanted to wait until we were officially married to have a physical relationship.

Of course, I wanted to be with her and sometimes the urge to touch her and feel her skin against mine was almost uncontrollable. But, she was the daughter of a preacher and I had to respect her values. So, we waited and that would make it so much sweeter when we were finally married.

By the time the movie was over I had lost track of how many glasses of scotch I drank, but when I noticed that my glass was empty I started to get up and pour another. I was drunk! I was too drunk to walk across the room to the bar. I hadn't eaten all day and I really don't know how much scotch I'd had. I just wanted to get back in the recliner and close my eyes. The room was spinning and I couldn't navigate my way around the coffee table. I stubbed my toe on the leg of the table and if I hadn't been so drunk I probably would have screamed in pain. I'm pretty sure my toe was broken. I saw the sectional sofa through the tears welling up in my eyes and I tried to flop myself on to it. I missed. This time I smashed my head and shoulder on the coffee table and landed on the floor, wedged between the table and sectional. I closed my eyes to stop the room from spinning. My head hurt and I felt sick to my stomach. At some point, I passed out.

VI

The throbbing pain in my foot is probably what woke me up. I had no idea where I was or why I was in such pain. Had I been in a fight? A car wreck? I slowly lifted my head and rotated it to the right. I could barely see the TV from under the table and I started to remember what was going on. I wondered what time it was? I went to push myself up and the pain in my shoulder was horrible. I finally got to my feet and hobbled toward the bathroom. My eyes were blurry and swollen and I could barely see. I glanced to the backyard and noticed it was almost dark. What in the hell time was it? How long had I been out?

Apparently, I had pissed myself while I was passed out. I flipped on the light in the bathroom and looked at myself in the mirror. I was expecting a bump on my head from hitting the table on the way down, but it was worse than I thought. I had cut my head open and blood had streaked down my face and into my eyes while I was out. Good Lord, I was a mess.

I needed a warm shower and something to eat. I started upstairs when I heard a knock at the front door. There was no way I could answer the door looking like this, with blood all over my face and piss stained shorts. But the lights in the kitchen were on and I couldn't make it from the top of the stairs, across the dining room and to the hallway to my room without someone at the front door seeing me. I hid on the stairs as someone knocked again. Crap! My only choice was to use the shower in the downstairs bathroom.

I stepped out of the shower, wrapped a towel around my waist, and looked at myself in the mirror again. The cut above my left eyebrow really wasn't that bad. Maybe all the alcohol in my system had thinned my blood or something because a cut that small shouldn't have bled as much as it did. I was definitely going to have some bruising around my eye socket. There was also bruising on my shoulder and my toe was still throbbing. I figured it was probably safe to head upstairs now so I gathered my stuff and on my way to the stairs, I saw my phone lying on the side table.

I had missed a call from Erin! God, I can't believe how stupid I am! Now she's probably worried about me. I had also missed a call from my mom.

Erin had replied to my earlier text with the picture of the TV.

Wow, that looks awesome! You're going to have such a great time living there this year.

As I got myself ready in the bathroom, I turned on the speakerphone and listened to my voicemails.

"Hey Rob, its Erin. I've been hanging out with some fellow first-year law students today. We had a great time and we're all going out to dinner together tonight. You're probably out having a great time in the big city. Why don't you try to give me a call tomorrow? Unless you just can't pull yourself away from watching movies on your own personal movie screen! I'm so jealous! Well, have a great evening. I'll talk to you tomorrow."

God, if she only knew the pathetic truth! Who were these fellow students? How did she meet them? What could they have been doing that was so important she couldn't take my call? And, now she's going out to dinner with them tonight? It sounds like law school is going to be like her sorority all over again.

"Hey Robbie, it's your mother. I hope you got all settled in. You're probably out at a sports bar watching the Cardinal's game and having a great time. If you're drinking, I want you to be very safe driving home. Call a cab if you need to. There's no need to take chances. Your dad and brother said to tell you hi. I love you and I'll talk to you tomorrow."

I had to laugh. A cab would have been nice to get me to the couch earlier. I was supposed to have new employee orientation at Edward Jones in three days. I was going to look absolutely wonderful in my photo for my employee ID badge.

I finally looked at the time. It was 8:30. I must have been passed out for about four hours and I was starving. Since I spent my afternoon getting drunk, I didn't go get any groceries and I really didn't want to go anywhere now. Hopefully Ambassador Nichols had some food somewhere in the house or I'd be ordering a pizza.

Lucky for me, the deep freeze in the laundry room was packed full. However, I was starving now and didn't want to wait for rib eyes to thaw out. There was a bag of frozen, jumbo shrimp. That would be perfect. They would thaw quickly. I put the shrimp in the sink with some running water and went outside to light the grill.

I couldn't see into the neighbor's back yard, but I could hear music and could tell that there were quite a few people over there. There was lots of laughing and jumbled conversation. It was probably slacker kid's slacker friends. Or, maybe bimbo invited everyone from the club. In any event, I confirmed my first impression of meathead. He was just a spoiled rich kid partying at mom and dad's mansion while they were out of town. He appeared to be about 25 or 26 years old and had probably been doing this since he was in high school.

I thought about how much Erin and I had accomplished in the past eight years since we met, and we did it all without rich parents. It was such a shame that this kid had every opportunity in the world and he was wasting his life and accomplishing nothing. It made me sick to think about people like him and their absolute disregard for hard work and self-reliance. And, here was a whole swarm of them, together in one place, wasting their lives.

I lit the grill and went back inside to find kabobs for the shrimp. They were nearly thawed so I put two dozen on sticks and found some Tony Chachere's Cajun seasoning in the panty. Uncle Rich had introduced us to the seasoning that summer that we visited him when

I first met Erin. It was great stuff and I put it on everything.

I put the shrimp on the grill and remembered my earlier plan to sit in the pool or the hot tub and watch the Cardinal's game through the patio doors on the 110-inch TV. While the shrimp cooked, I went back to my room and found my swim trunks. I was going to salvage the rest of this day.

Despite my earlier drunken stupor, I was feeling pretty good and I didn't think I could eat grilled shrimp without a beer to wash them down. So, for better or worse, I was going to start on round two. Just no scotch this time.

It was already in the sixth inning of the game by the time I got it turned on. It was still pretty warm outside, but I found a spot on the stairs of the pool and with my plate of shrimp and cold beer, I settled in to watch. I had a perfect view of the TV from where I was sitting and only wished that I had brought a whole cooler of beer with me.

"Hey. Hey, buddy. Over here."

I couldn't figure out who was talking. Were they talking to me? I looked around and couldn't see anyone.

"Hey buddy, over here. It's me, your neighbor."

Oh God. I didn't want to talk to this guy. He was probably going to ask me not to call the police later when his party gets loud and out of control. He was standing on the other side of the wrought iron fence that separated the two properties. The fence and a row of thick evergreen trees made it nearly impossible to see from one yard into the other. And yet, here was meathead, standing on the other side of the fence talking to me.

"Yeah, what do you need?"

"Hey, come over here. I want to introduce myself."

I got up and walked around the pool and across the yard toward the fence. Sure enough, there was slacker, douche-bag, meathead who was out in the driveway earlier today.

"Hey, my name's Brad. I'm your neighbor. I think I saw you looking out the window earlier today."

"Yeah, I was looking for something upstairs and was just admiring the view of the golf course."

"So, what's your name? Are you related to Mr. Nichols?"

"My name's Rob. No, we're not related. I'm just house-sitting for him."

"Well hey Rob, nice to meet you." He said as he stuck his hand through the fence.

I reached down to shake his hand, "Yeah Brad, nice to meet you too."

"Hey, I knocked on your door earlier. I was just going to let you know that I'm having a few friends over to celebrate the end of summer. You're more than welcome to come join us."

"Oh, thanks anyway. I've had a long day getting moved in and I think I'm just going to relax and head to bed early."

"That sounds great. Rest up because we'll be here tomorrow night too. You have to come join us tomorrow night."

"Okay, we'll see."

"Hey, there's no work on Monday. It's the end of the summer. You've got to come over and celebrate a little. One of my friends is going to roast a whole hog. By the middle of the day it's going to smell so good over here. The neighborhood's gonna be salivating all afternoon."

"Okay, thanks for the invite. Maybe I'll come over tomorrow

night."

"Great, see you then. Nice to meet you Rob."

"Nice to meet you Brad."

There was no way I was going to a party at his parent's house! The police would probably show up and everyone there will end up in jail. Hopefully his parents will be back after this weekend and I won't have to deal with living next door to an episode of *Cops* for the next year.

The Cardinals were blowing out the Padres and my curiosity got the best of me. I took as many beers as I could carry and headed back up to the attic to spy on Brad and his guests. I made sure to leave the lights off so they couldn't see me.

I couldn't see the back of the house, only the driveway and one corner of the pool. Brad and few other guys were standing around the car that he was working on earlier. I could practically guess what they were saying.

"Dude, sweet ride."

"Yeah, I know. I rebuilt the engine myself. You know, souped it up a bit. Took a stock engine and made it into a real dragster. This baby's got 700 horses under the hood."

"No way Bro. That's rad."

"Hey woman! Bring me and my friends another beer."

"So who's the new chick, Brad?"

"Oh, her. This is hilarious, but I can't even remember her name. I met her at the club last night, but for lunch she made me a sandwich while wearing a bikini."

"No way, dude. That's flippin' awesome. She's a keeper."

"Yeah, I know. I just need to figure out her name sometime before our wedding day."

And…laughter all around.

God, what a bunch of douche-bags! My whole life I've been surrounded by douche-bags. These guys were just like the frat boys in college and just like the jocks in high school. The only difference is that these guy's parent's have money. Otherwise they'd be working at the farmer's elevator back in Shelbyville like the big, bad, popular, douche-bag, football guys from high school.

My self-awareness and introspection could, at times, almost be a curse. My intelligence and maturity meant that I had very few peers in my younger years. I don't know if my intelligence was intimidating to the kids in Shelbyville, or if they just couldn't find a way to relate to me. The older I got, I kept hoping that I would gravitate towards people with a like IQ, and hopefully when I start my job on Tuesday that will be the case. However, I wasn't likely to find my peers next door.

I sat and watched them out the window for a few hours until I was out of beer. I had a lot of fun amusing myself by making up their dialog, although I'm sure my made up version was pretty close to the truth. I was drunk again and I was thinking about Erin.

Something, probably the alcohol, made me think that calling her at midnight would be a good idea. I dialed her number and it went straight to voicemail. I looked out the window one more time. The party next door was still going strong. I leaned my head back against the wall and closed my eyes and for the second time in one day, I passed out.

VII

I woke up lying on the hard, wooden floor of the attic. I tried to stretch and kicked over almost a dozen empty beer bottles. I hurt all over my body. Partly from sleeping on a wooden floor, but mostly from my little drunken episode the day before.

Today was going to be a better day. I would cook a healthy breakfast and then go for a drive. I needed to figure out how long it would take me to get to my office from here. I gathered up the empties and started down the stairs when I heard someone banging on the front door.

Who in the hell could it be at this time of day? It was probably the police. They were probably analyzing the crime scene next door and wanted to know what I had witnessed last night. I left the empty beer bottles on the attic stairs and went down to answer the door.

It was Brad! Only he had traded in his *TapOut* get-up from yesterday for a frat-boy, douche-bag, golf rig complete with plaid shorts and a visor. He looked ridiculous.

"Hey neighbor. Sorry to bother you so early in the morning. I was hitting golf balls in my backyard and one of them got away from me. I think it landed in your pool."

"Okay. Well you can go get it if you need to."

"I don't necessarily need it. I just wanted to let you know if you saw it in there that it came from me."

"Okay, I'll check it out later today and if I find it I'll toss it back in your yard."

"Great. Thanks. Hey, are you a golfer? A few of my friends and I are heading over to the country club. We're going to have brunch and then play a round. Are you interested in joining us?"

"No, I'm not really much of a golfer. I don't even have any clubs."

"I have an extra set of clubs. You're welcome to use them. It'll be a good time. Brunch will even be on me."

"Thanks anyway. I have a few things I need to do today."

"Okay, but we'll see you later tonight for the party, right?"

"I'm still thinking about it. It kind of depends on if I get everything done that I need to do."

"Okay, well I'll plan on seeing you later."

I'm sure his parents just loved that fact that he used their country club membership while they were out of town. Brad and his gang of douche-bags pretending to be high society with all the elderly couples having brunch after church was a funny thing to think about. I wonder if the country club served Jagermeister Bombs with Sunday brunch.

I immediately went outside and found his stupid golf ball lying next to the edge of the pool. I aimed toward his backyard and threw it as far as I could. Now he had no reason to knock on my door again.

After breakfast I went for a drive. I tried calling Erin again and again it went to her voicemail. I found the office without any problem. It would only take me 15 minutes to get there, even with traffic. I thought about driving straight to Columbia to see what was going on with Erin when my mom called.

"Hey Robbie, how are you doing?"

"I'm great mom. Just running a few errands."

"Have you found your office yet?"

"Yep, I just came from there. Now I'm going to get some groceries."

"You didn't do that yesterday? What did you do? I tried calling you."

"No, I didn't get groceries yesterday. I just put my stuff away and familiarized myself with the house."

"Oh, that's good. Did you go out to watch the Cardinal's game?"

"No, I just stayed here and fell asleep early."

"So what are your plans for today?"

"I don't know. I'll probably just hang around the house and go swimming."

"That sounds great. You know your father and I are proud of you Robbie. We know you'll do great at work."

"Thanks mom.

"Hey, by the way, did you happen to talk to Mrs. McMillen at church this morning?"

"Yes, briefly I talked to her and Reverend McMillen after church services."

"Did they mention going to Columbia to see Erin yesterday?"

"No, they didn't say anything about it. In fact, I'm pretty sure they were home all day. Why do you ask?"

"Just curious. Hey mom, I'm at the grocery store. I've gotta let you go."

"Okay, well enjoy your last few days of freedom before you start your career."

"Thanks mom. Talk to you later."

"I love you Robbie."

Shit! I really wanted to drive to Columbia and see her. I knew her parents didn't go there yesterday, she told me she was out with her new law school friends. But, she also told me she would talk to me today. Why didn't she answer?

I really didn't feel like getting groceries. I felt like going back home and getting drunk again. I remember the first time I ever drank. Of course, it was with Erin.

****

We had gone to a party with a big group of kids while we were juniors in high school. It was down by the creek on Mike Foster's parent's farm. We all drove our cars across the pasture and parked them and walked down to the sandbar by the creek.

It was actually about a week before the end of our junior year and the graduating seniors were throwing the party, but most of the underclassmen were there. I had always heard about these parties, but had never gone. Erin and I actually had planned a date that night. I was going to take her to dinner and a movie in Kirksville, but at the last minute she said that all of her friends were going to the party and we should just do that.

I had no intention of drinking and I really never thought I'd see Erin drink. But Marty Caldwell had a few mason jars full of something that he said was his dad's homemade peach wine. Erin brought me a jar and said it was really good. She took a drink in front of me as if to prove her point. I couldn't believe she was drinking! But if that's what she wanted to do on our date, then I would too.

Talk about burning on the way down! I thought peach wine would be sweet. This stuff smelled like rubbing alcohol. I don't really remember much from that night, like how I got home. I just remember that when my mom woke me up the next morning to catch the bus for the district track meet my car wasn't in the driveway.

"Robbie, where's your car?" my dad asked.

"Um. Um, it's at David's house. We were all out riding around last night and I just had David drop me off here rather than go to his house and get my car and then come back. I was afraid I might miss curfew."

"Miss curfew? David dropped you off before 10:00 last night."

"Yeah, well I just wanted to get home and get to bed so I would be ready for the track meet today. I'll get my car when I get back. Can you give me a ride to the school to catch the bus?"

I had to ask the guys on the track team where my car was. I really had no idea. That was the worst track meet I had ever run. I threw up twice before my first race. I had gone to state my sophomore year in both the mile and two mile. My junior year I finished fourth in both races and didn't qualify for state.

My parents never said anything, but I think they knew. Dad decided that the day after the track meet would be a great work day on the farm, at least for me.

As I was clearing brush that day I vowed that I would never drink again, and I didn't, for about five months. Erin and I had gone to every previous homecoming dance with groups of friends instead of as a couple, that's just the way the kids at our school did things. I really thought that for our senior year we might go together, but in the end we just all went as a big group again.

Erin had been voted homecoming queen and the king was going to be announced at the dance. Usually a football player was the homecoming king and I figured that this year wouldn't be any different. Although I called the football guys meatheads, I did have a few friends on the team and I wouldn't really care if one of them was the king and had their picture taken with Erin. But, no, the stupid redneck kids in my school voted for the biggest, stupidest redneck jock of all, Steve.

Steve had been a thorn in my side since the first time I met him. His mother and my mom volunteered often at church and school events and I guess you would call them friends. They thought it would be a good idea to get us together for play dates when we were young. That would have been a good idea if I had a limited vocabulary like Steve, but even at three years old I knew quite a few more words than hunting, farming and football.

Fourteen years later, Steve's vocabulary hadn't improved much, but for some reason he was the most popular kid in town. I guess that's what really cemented the fact that I had no peers in high school. If they could worship a guy like Steve Everton, how could they possibly relate to me?

Of course the king and queen had to dance. I was so pissed off. And I could tell that Erin didn't like it either. Steve had his big, greasy, meat hook hands on her. I'm sure she couldn't wait for that dance to be over. I never talked to her about it. I didn't want her to have to relive it.

My friend Casey had snuck some whiskey into the dance and was passing it around at the back table. It came to me and I decided what the heck? Maybe a little whiskey would make this night better. After the dance everyone went to Chris Youngblood's house for an after-party. We all ended up down by the woods having a bon fire. Casey had another bottle of whiskey and I don't remember much of the after-party.

By the end of our senior year, I was a drinking pro. I missed going to state again my senior track season, but by that time I really didn't care. I was just ready to get out of this town and move forward with the plan. I was so sick and tired of all the meatheads in school constantly flirting with Erin. I was ready to be alone with her in Columbia.

Our senior prom should have been the culmination of four years of high school dating for Erin and me. In the end she just wanted to go to prom with a big group of friends. She wasn't even concerned about my tux matching her dress. Luckily for me I heard Mrs. McMillen talking to my mom one day and talking about the gold sequin dress that Erin was going to wear. So, of course, we matched on prom night.

At the dance she kind of ran around and did her thing and I hung out with some friends of mine. It came time to announce the prom king and queen and I was kind of thinking it might be us. They made the announcement and sure enough, Erin was the prom queen, but once again, the king was Steve. I couldn't believe it! How could they not vote for a couple as king and queen? Fortunately, Casey once again supplied the whiskey.

****

I didn't end up getting any groceries. I went home and parked the car in the garage. I went to the basement and poured myself a scotch and sat in the recliner. I tried to call Erin again and again it went to voicemail. Pretty soon I was on my fourth scotch when I heard another knock at the door.

VIII

I really hoped it wasn't Brad again trying to invite me to his stupid, douche-bag party. I went upstairs and answered the door. Sure enough it was Brad.

"Hey, sorry to bother you again, but Ambassador Nichols has a folding table that he keeps in his garage and has let me borrow a few times. Do you think it would be okay to borrow it again for the party tonight?"

"Um, I don't know. I don't feel comfortable loaning out his stuff."

"You know, I would just go buy one of my own, but we're really busy getting stuff ready and I don't want to have to leave to go get one. I promise, I'll bring it back cleaner than it is now."

Apparently he wasn't going to take no for an answer. What could it hurt? It was just a stupid folding table. Even if Brad and his gang of hoodlums destroyed it, I'm sure Ambassador Nichols wouldn't miss a folding table.

"Okay, I'll open the garage."

"Here it is, right where I put it away last time. Hey, do you think you could help me carry it over to my house?"

God, this asshole was intrusive! Let me borrow your stuff that isn't really yours. Help me carry it to my house! Where were all of his little, douche-bag flunkies to help him carry it?

"Yeah, let me get some shoes on and I'll help you."

At this point I was willing to do whatever I had to in order for him to leave me alone. I grabbed one end and he grabbed the other and we carried the table across the lawn and around the corner of the house to his open garage.

There was that car from yesterday that had been sitting in the driveway. And the rest of the three-car garage was filled with a motorcycle, a black Land Rover and a silver BMW 235 convertible.

"How do you decide which one you're going to drive each day?" I joked, knowing that the motorcycle, Land Rover and BMW were probably his parent's vehicles.

"Well, I've been driving the Beemer for the past few years, but I just got the Nova finished up this week, so I plan on driving it quite a bit."

Just like I thought. He probably saved up his allowance and put a new stereo in it. Next he was going to tell me all about this quadrophonic Blaupunkt and the trunk full of sub-woofers. He got me over here, so I was going to have a little fun putting this douche-bag in his place.

"Oh yeah, what did you have done with the car?"

"Well, this was my dad's car. It's a 1973 Chevy Nova. He had bought it before he joined the military and left it in his dad's barn with plans to completely restore it when he got out of the service. By the time he got out of the army he was married to my mom. Pretty soon after that I was born. This wasn't really practical as a family car, so he sold it. He and my mom were on their way to drop it off to the buyer when they were hit by a drunk driver and were killed."

Of course, I knew it. He was a trust fund baby. His parents probably had a ton of life insurance and he got it when he turned 21 and has been burning through it ever since. He was probably almost broke.

"Wow, I'm sorry to hear that. So how did you end up with the car?"

"Well after my parents died, I was raised by my grandparents. My parents were pretty young when I was born and didn't have anything to speak of except this car. My grandparents didn't have much either, farming in those days wasn't what it is today you know, but my grandpa always kept this wrecked car in the barn out at the farm. He thought that maybe someday he would fix it up for me when I turned 16."

This wasn't making any sense. This guy is trying to tell me that his parents died and left him nothing and his grandparents were dirt poor farmers?!? He must have sold their farm in order to buy this house and his toys.

"My grandpa never got a chance to fix up the car. He died when I was 14 and grandma had to sell the farm. She just couldn't keep up with everything by herself. Our entire family history had to be sold at auction and a few family heirlooms that remained were put in a storage unit by my grandma."

That explains it. She must have had some heirlooms that turned out to be valuable and he sold them all. I was still confused. A few trinket heirlooms couldn't explain this house. He's got to be upside down in his mortgage. Or, maybe he's just renting until the money runs out.

"So, do you live here by yourself?" I asked, trying to pry a little and make some sense of what I was hearing.

"Just me and my wife, Kristy. And a little one on the way. But don't tell anyone. We're not quite ready to share that with anyone just yet."

Wow! Didn't I feel privileged? He and the club bimbo were

having a baby douche-bag and he told me first. I had to know more so I kept asking questions.

"So, if you don't mind me asking, what do you do for a living Brad?"

"Well, after high school I joined the army. My grandma had no money to send me to college and honestly, I'm not really the school type. While I was in the army I got deployed to Afghanistan. If you think it's hot here, you should try the Afghan desert wearing 80 pounds of army gear."

"Yeah, a few of the guys from back home joined the military right out of high school. I haven't seen them since graduation so I'm not sure if they were deployed or not."

"Well, you should get in touch with their parents and find out. You have no idea what it's like over there. If they are deployed, they would love to hear from friends back home.

"Anyway, I did my tour and came back home. I wasn't really sure what I wanted to do next, but for some reason I considered possibly being a personal trainer. I got a job at a local gym and was studying to get my license and I kept noticing how great my workout clothing was.

"I know that sounds really weird, but honestly, I could work out for two hours and be drenched in sweat and my clothes would be completely dry. One night I was sitting at home thinking about how awesome it would have been to have this type of clothing in Afghanistan; and my military apparel company was born. One year later I had a contract with the Department of Defense and two years after that I sold the company to Under Armour.

"I know. It's completely insane. I'm just kind of a good ole boy from the farm who planned on doing blue collar work the rest of my life and all of a sudden I'm sitting in a board room with Kevin Plank, the CEO of Under Armour, and getting a check for more money than I thought I would make in twenty lifetimes."

I didn't know what to say. I didn't know if he was full of shit or really being serious. About that time the back door opened and out walked the bimbo; I mean Kristy.

"Rob, this is my wife Kristy. She's the best thing that has ever happened to me. Kristy, this is our neighbor, Rob."

We exchanged pleasantries, but it didn't change my opinion of her. So what if Brad invented something all by himself and then sold it and got rich overnight? He was still a douche-bag, meathead and I'm sure she was a gold-digging bimbo that he drug home from the club after he made his millions.

"Rob, this girl right here took pity on me my freshman year of high school and accepted my invitation to the homecoming dance. I was an awkward 15 year old and she was the sweetest, nicest girl I had ever met. We ended up sitting next to each other in study hall and she not only went to that dance with me, but she helped me pass algebra and probably graduate high school. She's the only girlfriend I've ever had and we've been together ever since.

"Even while I was deployed and she was in college. We wrote letters and then kept up with each other through Facebook. As soon as I got back we got married and moved in together. I had zero job prospects and had a crazy idea that I thought I could be a personal trainer.

"Kristy was level headed and just kept moving forward with her plan and went to law school at Wash U. I did my best to support us during that first year of marriage and I kept wondering why she stayed with me. In the end, she negotiated the sale to Under Armour.

"And now" He said as he placed his hand on her stomach. "She's going to have my baby!"

My head was spinning. Maybe I was drunk again. This guy had to be so full of crap. Erin and I were the only couple I knew that had been together since our freshman year of high school. And for him to say that his wife went to law school at Wash U! It was just too unbelievable. Who were these people?

About that time two guys walked up from somewhere in the back yard.

"Rob, these are my friends, Scott and Jay. They're roasting the hog that we're going to have tonight. How's it coming along guys? It smells great."

"It'll be done on time." Said one of them.

"Nice to meet you Rob." Said the other. "Hey Brad, what time is Frank supposed to get here with the sound equipment?"

Oh, the sound equipment. So, I was going to be kept awake all night with the head-banger music that self-made millionaire Brad was going to project all over the neighborhood with Frank's 'sound equipment.'

"He said he would be here around 4:00. Hey Rob, what kind of music do you listen to?"

I don't really listen to music. It isn't something that interests me. But I had to say something.

"Oh, I guess I like a mix; some country, a little classic rock and even a little blues and classical."

"Well, I think you're going to love this tonight. Have you ever heard of King Crown?"

"No, I don't think so. What do they sing?"

"Well, what *we* sing is Christian Rock, said Jay. "The three of us, along with our friend Frank from church started a band. We're going to play here tonight."

This was getting weirder by the minute. I kept expecting Erin to come out from behind the garage with Ashton Kutcher and tell me that I was being punked.

"Yeah, you know, when I sold my company to Under Armour it was partly because they offered me a great deal. But, it was also because I just didn't feel fulfilled in what I was doing. I felt like there was more that I should be doing. I hadn't been to church since I joined the army and I really missed it.

"Since selling the company I now volunteer for the church as a youth pastor. It's honestly the most fulfilling work I've ever done."

"Hey honey, said bimbo, I mean, lawyer-wife Kristy. "Tell him about the church youth camp."

"Oh yeah. So after I sold the company the first thing I wanted to do was buy back my grandparent's farm. However, all but 60 acres of the original 300 acre farm had already been developed. So, I bought the remaining 60 acres.

"I'm currently having it developed as a camp for the kids from church and I'm going to name it after my grandparents. It's going to be great. But, the best part is that the remaining 60 acres included the original barn. And, inside that barn is where my grandfather had stashed this car. I finally got it, had it restored and I plan on driving it until I can give it my grandkids."

This was, without a doubt, the craziest thing I had ever heard. If I wasn't drunk already, then I really needed a drink. I told my neighbors and their friends that I was expecting a phone call and had left my phone at home, but I would definitely be back later tonight. I had to tell Erin about this. She would get a kick out of it and might even drive down tonight to attend this 'party' with me.

There was no way that I was buying all the crap that I had heard. I remember Reverend McMillen telling the joke many times;

"Why do you have to take two Baptists' fishing with you? Because if you only take one he'll drink all your beer."

I was perfectly aware of those who overtly claimed to walk in the footsteps of Jesus and those who claimed to be born-again Christians. True Christians kept their beliefs to themselves. They don't feel the need to talk about how holy and wholesome they are. It was the born-again's that you had to watch out for. Generally, they had something to hide and they hid it behind their religion.

I was definitely going to Brad's party tonight and I was going to catch 'Holy Man' and his friends and his bimbo wife in less than holy behavior. Maybe I would even snap a few pictures on my phone and bring down the whole charade.

IX

I got back to the house and had to pour myself another drink. I sat down in the recliner and tried to digest everything I had heard. Let's see if I have all of this straight. The dirt poor, dumb as a box of rocks, douche-bag, army kid stumbles on a great idea and sells it to Under Armour and makes millions. The bimbo with a heart of gold has been his girlfriend since they were freshmen in high school and is now a lawyer who negotiated a multi-million dollar deal with a publicly traded company. After douche-bag makes his millions he decides that he is going to be a man of the cloth and is building a church camp on the property that used to be his grandparent's farm, that he bought back from the greedy developers just in the nick of time to save it. And just to put a little icing on the cake, he found his father's original 1973 Chevy Nova, that his parents died in when hit by a drunk driver, in the barn out at the farm and was able to restore it to its original glory. And how could I forget, he and his douche-bag buddies are in a Christian Rock band!

Uh, yeah, Erin has to hear this. I picked up my phone and dialed her number.

"Hey Rob, how are you? How's everything at the mansion in the big city?"

"Erin, you're not going to believe this story. I just met my neighbor. He told me a story that is the most unreal thing you have ever heard," I said and proceeded to tell her what had just transpired.

"Wow, Rob, that's pretty amazing. I bet you're going to meet all

59

kinds of amazing people at work and in your neighborhood."

Amazing? These people aren't amazing. Is she even listening to me? They're con men. How can she not see that?

"Hey, Erin, this Brad guy, the born-again, multi-millionaire army guy is having a party tonight and he invited me. Why don't you come down to St. Louis and go with me? You wouldn't want to miss this. Apparently there's going to be a whole-hog roast, a Christian Rock band and who knows what else."

"Oh, Rob, it sounds like you're going to have a great time. I hope you meet lots of new people. I just don't think I can make it."

I don't think she heard a single word I said. This wasn't about having a good time at a party and meeting new people. This is about bringing down a bunch of posers and I wanted her to be there with me.

"Erin, are you sure? I don't know if I like living two hours away. I never get to see you."

"I know Rob; it's going to be an adjustment. I just can't make it tonight. I have too many things to do to get ready for classes."

"Ok, well, one of these days soon you need to come to St. Louis. For the whole weekend. You need to see the house and we need to go out to dinner. I'll try out a few restaurants and pick out a good one for us."

"That sounds great Rob. I'm looking forward to it. Have a great time tonight and good luck at your new job on Tuesday."

X

Erin hung up her phone and set it down on the table. She turned her head toward Luke, who was sitting in the lounge chair next to her at the apartment complex swimming pool.

"That was my friend Rob from back home. He just graduated in May and moved to St. Louis and will be starting a job at Edward Jones this week. He thought we should come to St. Louis tonight to attend a party that he's been invited to at one of his new neighbor's.

"Rob has always been such a sweet guy. I think he had a crush on me when my family first moved to Shelbyville. A lot of kids at school were kind of mean to him because he's really awkward socially, but I always tried to be his friend. I'm not really sure, but I think at one time he might have taken medication for some sort of social anxiety syndrome or something like that. I remember overhearing my mom and his mom talk about it one time. He might still take it for all I know.

"He went to Mizzou also, and occasionally we studied together. I think all he really wanted was just to fit in and have friends. He's just always had a hard time interacting with people.

"Honestly, I was really surprised when he even went to college. I wasn't sure if his anxiety and awkwardness would even allow him to be able to do well around all those new people, but I was wrong. I think he seemed to do better once we got out of Shelbyville and he wasn't around the same people who had known him his whole life. He's just really quiet and shy and awkward. It's hard to describe."

"Well, listen Erin, if you want to go and visit your friend, that's fine with me. I'll even go with you if you want. I'd love to meet him. Or, you can just run down there if you'd rather visit with him by yourself."

"Luke, that's what I love about you. You're so understanding. I think we should definitely plan a trip to St. Louis very soon to go visit Rob. I think he would love to meet you also.

"I think I've kind of always felt like a sister to Rob. He's always been very protective of me and I'm just so happy that he finished college and has a job. I'm really proud of him and how far he's come. I think that if he can work in an environment with people who will give him a chance and not be judgmental about his idiosyncrasies, then I really feel like he'll do okay in life."

"Well anytime you want to go for a visit, you just let me know."

"Thanks sweetie. I love you." Said Erin as she leaned across her lounge chair and kissed Luke on the cheek.

XI

I hung up the phone and poured myself another scotch. What could she have going on that is so important that she can't come to a Labor Day party two hours away? Oh well, I was secure in our relationship and have no reason to question her motives. Next weekend she will be here. We will be living like royalty in our mansion. Just a little taste of what the future holds for us. Tonight, I was going to expose the douche-bag neighbors for what they really were.

I had a few hours to kill before I went back over to Brad's party and I may as well be sufficiently lit when I arrive. I took the last drink from my scotch, leaned back in the recliner and closed my eyes. I was smiling to myself as I imagined calling Brad out on his hypocrisy. Maybe a few pictures of the drunk-fest sent to Brad's church youth group would put him in his place. True, Erin wouldn't be here with me, but I was going to have fun tonight.

I tried to doze off, but kept thinking about Erin, back in Columbia, all by herself. Erin was a very attractive girl and I'm not just saying that because we're together. She got lots of attention in high school and all throughout college. She was smart and mature enough to handle it and was always polite to the boys who talked to her. But I know that her religious values had to be insulted by the ignorant comments that the rednecks back in Shelbyville and the douche-bag frat boys made to her.

****

I remember one douche-bag, frat boy in particular from college that was always hitting on her. His name was Randy and he was such a prick. I don't know what makes guys think they can just randomly hit on girls, especially ones who are in a relationship, but I made certain that he understood that his advances were unwelcome.

My first experience with Randy was during the first semester of our freshman year at Mizzou. Erin and I were supposed to meet at the library to study for a chemistry exam. I remember texting Erin to tell her that I'd see her there around 6:30. She replied back that it's Friday night and the exam isn't until next Wednesday. Why don't we meet on Sunday and study then?

I had never known Erin to blow off her school work and this was one of the first signs that her sorority was corrupting her. Apparently they had some homecoming skit and were partnered up with a fraternity, Randy's fraternity! I went to the library and studied for a few hours and texted Erin several times, pretending like I needed help with my chemistry. She didn't reply so I decided to go make sure she was okay.

I walked across campus to her sorority house, but no one was there. I walked back across campus to the fraternity section and started knocking on doors, asking if the girls from Alpha Chi Omega were there. I had several doors slammed in my face before someone finally told me that they were working on a homecoming skit with the Delta Chi's at the field house.

Thirty minutes later I was at the field house. There were hundreds of college students dressed up in the most ridiculous costumes I'd ever seen. The sight of their ignorance reinforced my first impression that Greek life wasn't for me. I walked through the crowd trying to find Erin, or at least someone from her sorority that I recognized. Finally, I saw a few girls that I recognized. I started to ask them where Erin was when I saw her, talking to some guy!

I walked behind a canvas stage prop so I could get closer without her seeing me. I just wanted to make sure she was okay and then I was going to leave. I didn't want her to think I was checking up on her. From behind the edge of the canvas I could hear them talking. Well, I could hear the guy. Erin really wasn't saying anything.

The douche-bag was talking all about some summer internship that he had done in New York. From what I could gather he was going to graduate in May and already had a job lined up with some big accounting firm in New York. Thank God! May couldn't get here soon enough to get this creep away from my girl.

Then he asked her what she was doing when they were done with rehearsal. He said that they were having a 'get-together' back at the frat house and she was welcome to join them.

That was it! I'd heard enough. I wasn't going to let this jerk take advantage of my sweet, innocent Erin by drugging and raping her back at his frat house. I came out from behind the canvas and punched him in the back of the head.

It was the first and only time I have ever punched anyone in my life and I can't believe how much it hurt my fist. I froze momentarily; partially because of the pain in my hand and partially because I thought that that would be it, one punch and I had saved Erin's honor. But when he turned around and looked at me and mouthed the words, "Who the hell are you?" I flew into a fit of rage.

I lunged at him and we ripped through the canvas and onto the floor. I had never fought before in my life and had no idea what I was doing, but I was giving it everything I had. People were yelling and hands were grabbing at me and I just kept wailing away, hoping to land a knockout blow.

Eventually I was pulled off of Randy. Unfortunately, he appeared to be unscathed, except for a little red swelling that was beginning under his left eye. His frat brothers had a hold of me and I'm afraid that if Erin hadn't stepped in, they might have let Randy get revenge before tossing me out on my head.

Erin was pissed! But we went outside and talked for a while.

She explained that part of being in a sorority is social functions and service projects and they usually get paired up with a fraternity and this is something that is going to continue throughout college.

I tried to tell her that I thought Randy was going to drug her and date rape her, but she assured me that that wouldn't happen. She had met Randy at several functions and he was always a gentleman.

We made an agreement that night that we would always study together at least twice a week and that I wouldn't crash any more sorority events, and I didn't. But I did keep an eye out for Randy on campus for the rest of that year and I did see him early the next week leaving a building that I was going into. I smiled to myself when I saw the purple bruise on his cheekbone, and then quickly ducked into my Calculus class before he saw me.

****

In any event, it was always difficult, knowing that jerks like Randy were everywhere and they had no qualms about walking up to some girl they had never met and just striking up a conversation. With Erin, being as beautiful as she is, I know it happens frequently, and for the foreseeable future I'm going to be two hours away. Who's going to stand up for her honor?

I finished another scotch and decided it was about time to get ready for Brad's party. I had no idea what I was going to wear, but I knew that it was going to be an eventful evening.

XII

I poured another scotch and took it upstairs with me to get dressed. I decided that khaki cargo shorts and a blue polo shirt would work just fine. I laid out my clothes and jumped in the shower.

I guess the scotch was starting to work its magic on me while I was showering because I started thinking that it would probably be a good idea to call and invite Erin again. I finished my shower and that's exactly what I did.

"Hey Rob, how's it going? Are you getting ready for your party?"

I didn't know what to say. I couldn't believe she actually answered. I wasn't prepared to actually speak to her.

"Rob? Rob? Did you mean to call me?"

"Um, uh, yeah I did. I just thought I'd check with you one last time before I head over to this party. You know it's really just right down the road. We'll have a great time."

"Rob, I know you're going to have a great time. I promise I will come to St. Louis soon and spend a weekend with you. I just can't do it this weekend."

"I know. I figured that's what you'd say. I just thought it wouldn't hurt to check one more time."

"Well thanks for checking and have a great time. I want to hear all about it."

"Okay, I'll give you a call tomorrow and tell you all about it."

"Sounds good. Goodnight Rob."

"Goodnight Erin.

"I love you", I whispered to the phone, after I knew she had already hung up.

I slammed the rest of my scotch and went downstairs to get another while I finished getting ready.

XIII

"That was Rob inviting me to the party in St. Louis again." Erin said to Luke.

"You know, maybe you should go. The poor guy is all alone in a new town. He's going to a party with a bunch of people he doesn't know. He needs his wingman, uh, wing-girl." Luke replied.

"Luke, I want to spend the weekend with you. Today was fabulous and we only have one more day to spend together."

"Actually, we don't Erin. I have a huge case on Tuesday that I have to prepare for. I probably should spend a few hours tonight and part of the day tomorrow working on it. That way I won't have to worry about it tomorrow afternoon when we go to visit my parents in Jeff City."

"I can't wait to meet your parents."

"And they can't wait to meet you. The fact that I am actually bringing a girl to meet them is a big step. They know I'm serious."

"Ahhh. Said Erin blushing. "I love you so much. I don't really want to be away from you."

"I know. But think how much it would mean to your friend if you went to this party with him. Then the two of you could grab breakfast in the morning and he can show you where he works and then you can head back. Hopefully, I'll be finishing up with my work by then. You know it will mean the world to him and all he wants is to show you his house and his office."

"I know. It would mean a lot to him."

"Just do it Erin. I really will work better and get more done if you're not here to distract me."

"Distract you? I don't distract you when you're working."

"I didn't mean distract me. I meant be a distraction to me. You know that if you're in the same apartment as me, I'm not going to want to work. I'm going to want to snuggle on the couch with you while you watch TV and then snuggle under the covers with you the rest of the time."

"I see. So what you're saying is it would be a big help to you if I wasn't around for the next 24 hours?"

"Well, maybe the next 18 hours. I wouldn't want you gone too long."

"Okay. You know what? I'm going to go visit my friend Rob!"

XIV

I was just finishing up shaving, and another scotch, when my phone rang. It was Erin.

"Hey Rob. Guess What?"

"What's that Erin?"

"I've had a change of plans. I'm coming to the party with you tonight. That is if the offer still stands and it's not too late."

"What? You are? I mean that's great. Of course the offer still stands. How soon are you leaving?"

"I am in my car and getting on the interstate right now. I'll be there in less than two hours. I hope that doesn't make you late for the party."

"No, no. That's great. It's only 6:00. That will be perfect. I'm going to text you the address so you can GPS it. I'll see you soon."

"Okay. I'm on my way."

Oh my God. I was freaking out. At least that would give me time to sober up a little bit. My room was a pig sty. I had no food in the house because I had never bought groceries. If Erin was going with me, then I couldn't show up empty handed. I needed to bring something to the party. Oh man. This changes everything. I can't believe it. I can't believe that the love of my life is on her way to St.

Louis to spend Labor Day weekend with me in this amazing house and go to an amazing party. I didn't have much time, but I had a lot to do to make this weekend perfect.

I really hadn't unpacked much yet, so I gathered my dirty clothes and threw them in the laundry room. I finished getting myself ready and decided to run to the store. I would need something to take tonight and also food for breakfast. And lunch? And possibly dinner tomorrow?

Luckily there was a grocery store only about six blocks away. I had no idea what to take to a party. I'd never been to anything like this. I ran up to the deli counter. There was a large, black woman working the meat slicer. She didn't look very happy to see me.

"Can I hep you?"

"Um, I'm going to a neighborhood party tonight and I need to take a dish with me. Can you suggest anything?"

"Wha' kinda party is it?"

"Um, I don't know? Are there different kinds of parties?"

"Yay. Dere's barbeque's. Dere's Mexican fiestas. Dere's tropical seafood parties. Dere's…."

"Um, it's a barbeque. The host is roasting a whole hog."

"Okay. Did they ax you to bring sumthin' dat go wit pok?"

"No. They didn't ask me to bring anything. I just didn't want o show up empty handed."

"Well, din it don' matta whatchu bring. Take some dessert. Dese creampuffs is good."

"Perfect. I'll take two dozen of those."

Wow. Not exactly the same as the local deli back home in Shelbyville, but pretty close to the Wal-Mart deli in Columbia. I decided I could handle breakfast food on my own. I then made the executive decision that if lunch and dinner tomorrow were involved then we would be going out to eat on Ambassador Nichols' crisp, new $100 bill.

Just as I was in the check-out line I saw the floral shop by the exit. Fresh flowers in the kitchen were exactly what I needed to greet Erin. Actually, a dozen roses on the formal dining room table and a dozen tulips on the kitchen island is what I decided.

I sped back home and pulled into the garage. I ran inside and put my groceries away. I found a platter to arrange my cream puffs and put those in the refrigerator. A vase of flowers on the table and one on the island. I looked down at my watch; it wasn't even 7:00 yet. I had a whole hour to kill! I really wanted a drink, but I was finally feeling sober from drinking earlier. Oh well, one more scotch wouldn't hurt. And while I'm at the bar, I should probably check the wine cellar for a bottle of chardonnay. I know that's what Erin likes and I have just enough time to get it chilled.

XV

I actually had time for three more scotches before I saw headlights pull into the driveway. It was 8:05. I don't know if she got lost or had to make a pit stop, but it took her longer than it should have.

I met her at the door and gave her a big hug.

"You can't even begin to understand how happy I am to see you. This is going to make this weekend perfect."

"That's sweet Rob. This house is amazing. I can't believe that you actually live here.

"I know. Me neither. Come on in and I'll give you the grand tour. Are you ready for a glass of wine?"

"Sure, that sounds great. Wow, these flowers are gorgeous." She said as we walked through the dining room toward the kitchen. I smiled to myself as I led the way.

"And so are these." She said as we entered the kitchen.

I pulled the bottle of chardonnay from the fridge and grabbed the cork screw from the drawer. I had no idea if the wine was any good, but I figured anything Ambassador Nichols has in his wine cellar is probably top shelf.

I had my scotch and Erin her glass of chardonnay and we toured the house. I'm pretty sure that she was impressed. I don't know if she was impressed enough to switch law schools, but I'm pretty sure that she would be coming back for frequent visits.

I had to show her the attic, where I first met the neighbors. When I opened the door to go upstairs, I completely forgot about the beer bottles that I had left there this morning when Brad rang the doorbell.

"I'm not really sure what's up with those. I saw them yesterday when I was exploring the house." I said as we made our way past the dozen or so empties and up the stairs.

From the window I pointed out the country club to the west and the party going on at Brad's house next door.

"Well, why don't you introduce me to your new friends Rob?"

"Sounds good. I'm going to grab something from the fridge and we'll get our drinks and head over."

XVI

As we walked across the front yard I noticed that cars were lined up on both sides of the street as far as I could see. They even went around the corner at the end of the block. There must have been 50 or 60 cars, which meant that there were probably at least 100 people here.

Erin and I walked down the driveway and around the corner of the garage. The place was packed! There was now a stage complete with sound system and set up for a band between the garage and the pool. A 30 foot long table held every side-dish you could imagine.

Brad saw us walk up and headed our direction.

"Wow! So you didn't tell me that you had a missus."

"Brad, this is Erin. Erin, this is Brad."

They exchanged pleasantries and Erin noticed the fleet of cars in the garage.

"Oh my gosh! I love that Beemer." She said

"You should talk Rob into giving you a tour of the city in it. Seriously, any time the two of you want to go for a ride, just let me know, it's all yours. I plan on driving the Nova till the wheels fall off."

"Absolutely! I would love to take it for a spin." She replied.

About that time Kristy walked up and took the platter of crème puffs from me and placed it near an assortment of desserts on the table.

"Hey sweetheart. This is Rob from next door. You remember him from earlier today? And this is Erin."

"Hey Erin," I said, "Kristy graduated from Wash U law school."

"Wow," said Erin, "That was one of my final three choices. I had several really good connections in Columbia and Jeff City and decided to stay at MU for law school."

"MU was actually my first choice," said Kristy, "But with Brad's business doing so well here, we decided at the time that we shouldn't leave St. Louis."

The girls immediately hit it off and were deep in conversation. Of course, Brad and Kristy were about six or seven years older than Erin and I, but I could see a lot of similarities in our relationships that I had missed earlier.

The barbeque boys, Scott and Jay were back.

"Hey Brad, the hog is done and is ready for presentation," said Jay.

"Hey Rob, can you give us a hand carrying it up?"

"Sure, no problem."

I set our alcohol down next to the table and whispered to Erin, "Hey, I'm going to go help these guys with the barbeque. I'll be back in a few."

"No problem, I'll be right here."

We walked deep across the back yard toward the far corner. The smell was amazing and I could see red-hot coals as soon as we were out of the light of the house.

"Erin seems like a really sweet girl," said Brad.

"She's amazing. We've been together since our freshman year in high school, just like you and Kristy. And, she's going to law school, just like Kristy."

"Pretty cool isn't it? To have an amazing woman, who you would lay down your life for, without even thinking twice."

I nodded my head and thought to myself, yes, it is absolutely the coolest thing in the world to have an amazing woman. My entire life for the past eight years has revolved around Erin. Although the thought of laying down my life for her had never really crossed my mind, I knew without a doubt, that if that's what it called for, that's what I would do.

XVII

We got to the back of the yard, where the red coals were glowing and found a make-shift fire pit, built from cinder blocks. There was a pile of aged oak and hickory firewood next to it and an expanded-metal grate on top. As we got closer I realized there were actually two expanded metal grates and sandwiched in between was a whole hog, spread-eagle, and seared perfectly.

"Man, I have always wanted to roast a whole hog," said Brad.

"Rob, this thing has been slow roasting since 8:00 this morning," said Jay.

"Well, it smells amazing."

Scott was busy undoing some sort of clip that held the two metal grates together.

"Everyone grab a glove and a corner." He said.

We lifted the top grate off and there was the whole hog lying on top of the bottom grate. Each grate had handles welded on and Scott instructed each of us to grab a corner. We hoisted the hog above our heads and made a ceremonial march back to the food table. A place was arranged to set the hog down and we arrived to thunderous applause and whistles.

I saw Erin out of the corner of my eye; glass of wine in hand, grinning ear to ear. She gave me a quick wink. This was the second best day of my life, only paling in comparison to the day we first met eight years ago.

We set the grate down on its designated spot on the table and Brad grabbed a carving knife and fork.

"Ladies and gentlemen," he announced. "Thank you all for being here to celebrate with us tonight. It is through God's graciousness that we are able to gather and enjoy one another's friendship and company. It is only through God's will that this food be blessed for the nourishment of our bodies. And it is through God's understanding that we can grow closer as friends and grow closer to our savior, Jesus Christ. Amen"

And with that, everyone raised their bowed heads and watched as Brad plunged his fork into the seared hog skin and began pulling the perfectly cooked hog. Pretty soon Jay handed me a pair of rubber gloves and said to dig in. Once the skin had been cut it was pretty much a rip and shred event as we pulled pork and placed it on platters. Of course, the cooks got to sample every other pull.

At one point while we were pulling pork, Erin brought me a glass of scotch. My hands were so greasy that there was no way I could hold a glass. She recognized this and held it up to my mouth and tipped.

I swallowed my drink and turned to dig back in to the hog and caught Brad looking at me and smiling. At that point he gave me a head nod and smiled his great big, good ole boy; I've got your back grin. Maybe I had misjudged him. Maybe I no longer cared about setting him up and seeing him fail. After all, tonight was all about Erin and me moving forward with the plan that we had made so many years ago.

XVIII

The evening was a blur. I had no recollection of time and really didn't care. Erin was amazing the way she flittered among the crowd and was able to carry on conversation. I became her wing-man, and I was okay with that.

Brad and Kristy continually introduced us to their friends as Rob and Erin, from next door. We met college students, financial planners, tattoo artists, body builders, preachers, teachers, attorneys, auto-mechanics and a few politicians. The ages ranged from early twenties to at least late fifties. Brad knew everyone and he introduced us as his new friends, and as a couple.

Pretty soon it was time for the King Crowns to play. Brad got on stage and announced into the microphone that everyone should find a seat and a sweetheart to snuggle with, because the music would begin shortly.

Kristy grabbed Erin by the arm and motioned for us to follow her. On the far side of the pool was a swing, wide enough for two.

"This is going to be the best seat in the house for the show." She said. "And I think you two should have it tonight."

It was an old-fashioned porch swing hung on a cedar arbor frame. It was at the opposite end of the swimming pool from the driveway and the food table and the stage.

Kristy was absolutely correct. The swing was perfect. Most everyone else tried to grab seats upfront or lounge chairs on either side of the pool. Our swing was just out of the reach of the ambient light from the house and the pool and there was really no one else around. A few sound checks occurred from the stage and just as they were about to start their first set Kristy reappeared with a blanket from the house.

"You may not need it now, but I just saw the weather and there's a front moving in. It's going to get chilly before the night's over."

The swing had a cushioned seat and back. It was surprisingly comfortable. I put my left arm across the back and held my scotch in my right hand. I was slowly rocking us back and forth when Erin picked her feet up from the yard and curled them underneath her and leaned her head over on my shoulder. She grabbed the blanket off the back of the swing and covered her legs.

If I happened to die at that moment, I would have died a happy man.

XIX

The show was amazing. I always thought that Christian Rock was music that born-again posers listened to in order to prove that they were really Christian. But, Brad and his band were great. This was stuff that I could actually listen to.

By the time they were done playing it was after midnight and I was afraid that Erin had fallen asleep on my shoulder. I know that I had moved my arm from the back of the swing to around her shoulders and I really didn't care if they played until the sun came up.

While Brad was thanking his guests for attending, Erin sat up and sighed a deep sigh. She looked at me and smiled.

"Did we bring my wine over here?" she said, "I think I could use another glass."

"We didn't, but I can go get it. I need another scotch anyway."

I got up and walked around the pool and back toward the garage where the food table was and where we had left our cooler of alcohol. People were starting to leave and there was quite a crowd in the area. I finally made my way to my cooler and saw Brad wishing his guests farewell and drive safe.

"Brad, that was amazing. I honestly think that you found your calling in that band."

"It all comes from the heart Rob. Anything you do that comes from the heart is bound to be good isn't it?"

"I suppose you're right. I have to tell you Brad, I had a different opinion of you yesterday. I'm glad you proved me wrong. I don't think we're really that different."

"I always enjoy proving people wrong. That's my specialty. As long as you had a good time tonight and you and your girl are closer than you were at the beginning of the night, then I accomplished my goal."

"Absolutely!" I replied.

By the time I got back to the swing to bring Erin her wine, Kristy was seated next to her and Erin had a drink in her hands.

"Hey Rob, Kristy brought me a glass of her favorite wine. Since she can't drink for the next six months she thought I might enjoy it."

I grabbed an Adirondack chair from the yard and pulled it up close. I set the cooler down and put my glass of scotch on the wide arm rest. As long as these two wanted to talk, I was willing to be a spectator.

I finished that scotch and then another. Pretty soon I looked at my phone and noticed it was 1:30 am and nearly everyone was gone. Brad and the band had loaded the sound equipment into a van and his friends left. He walked around the edge of the pool to join us and suggested that since it was really cooling off, we all go inside.

XX

The four of us made our way into Brad and Kristy's house. Erin poured another glass of wine and Brad grabbed a bottle from the kitchen counter.

"Rob, I noticed that you're a scotch man, but are you interested in trying a bourbon?"

"Sure, I just became a scotch man recently. I'm not real familiar with bourbon, but I'll give it a try."

"This is Booker's. It's a single barrel bourbon and one of my favorites," he said as he poured us each a glass.

Kristy asked Erin if she was interested in seeing the nursery, and of course she was.

As Kristy and Erin headed down the hallway, Brad and I pulled up bar stools to the island in the kitchen. I'd been drinking scotch for two days straight and the bourbon certainly was different. It burned on the way down, just like the scotch, but with a different flavor.

"Isn't it crazy? Just life in general I mean. It's like this huge blank canvas that we are given and we can paint whatever we want on it. And we start painting, thinking we know what we're doing, and all of a sudden we think we're painting a tree and it starts looking like a mountain. And before long it is a mountain, because we thought the tree was important, but it was just a small detail in the much bigger picture. It's just crazy. There has to be a higher power guiding all of it."

Brad was spewing poetic, philosophic, religious talk and strangely, I was listening and I was in agreement. Of course, he was a fly-by-the-seat-of-your-pants kind of guy and he didn't know about my life plan, but he was still making a lot of sense. I had already painted a scene for Erin and me and her decision to stay in Columbia and not come to St. Louis with me meant that the scene was going to change just a bit. I was still coming to grips with the reality of the whole situation, but this weekend just reinforced what I had known for the past eight years - Erin and I were meant to be together and I wouldn't let anyone stand in the way of that. Earlier in the evening Brad mentioned laying down his life for his wife. I took that to heart and I knew that not only would I lay down my life for Erin, but I would also be prepared to take the life of anyone who tried to come between the two of us.

I had never really thought of it in quite those terms. Erin and I had always been secure in our relationship. But, I also knew that she endured the constant barrage of douche-bags who hit on her. I made up my mind right then and there that I wouldn't tolerate another Steve or Randy trying to interfere with our relationship. It was time to be a man and protect what was mine.

"Don't you ever just wish you could paint exactly what was in your head, and that would be it?" I replied.

"No, honestly I don't. I mean, having goals and ideas and a thing that we work toward is great. My Christian youth camp is one of those things. But, I have no desire to know what's going to happen next year or in 20 years or how my life is going to end. God already has that planned anyway. What good would it do to know? That's all part of the mystery and surprise that life entails."

"I've never been much for surprises. I like to have a plan. I like when I have a plan in my head and everything works out according to plan. Of course, I understand that there may be some unexpected things that occur that are better than what we had planned, but for the most part, I enjoy knowing that I am the captain of my ship."

"But the thing is, you're not captain of your ship. God is the captain and he knew before you were ever born what your destiny would be."

"If that's the case and you honestly believe it, then why are some people destined to a life of poverty? Or a life of crime? Why would God bring people into this world only to live a life of suffering and hardship?"

"I still believe that God gives us free will. He creates us in his image as imperfect humans. Life gives us choices. God doesn't control human interaction, he creates us and he knows how we are going to respond to each choice we are faced with. I think that some of his creations are meant to be examples to the rest of us. Good and bad examples. The bible gives us direction on how to respond to real life, but it's up to us to make the decision of how we actually will respond."

"Possibly. I just like the idea of being in control of as much as I can."

"And you are in control. It's just that God knows and has always known how you will respond to everything you encounter. Your life isn't an island. The choices you make affect those around you, just like their choices affect you. God placed you on earth for a reason. It's up to you to figure out why."

About that time the girls came back in the kitchen.

"Just what we need. Drunken philosophy!" said Kristy

"That's one of my favorite games," replied Erin.

"Why don't we sit somewhere more comfortable? What do you think Brad? Do you think they would want to watch the video of the church camp being built?"

"What do you think guys? Until we have this baby, the church camp video is the only one we can show you that you would rather not watch, but will probably sit politely through, especially if there's alcohol involved."

"Why not? It's only two in the morning, we live next door and we have no plans tomorrow. Let's watch a church camp video!" I said.

XXI

Brad and Kristy's basement was almost exactly like Ambassador Nichols'. They had a huge rec room with a giant TV and a sectional sofa. There was a bar in the corner and a fitness room.

Erin and I found a spot on the sectional and Brad poured us each another drink while Kristy navigated the menu on the TV to find the video she wanted. We all settled in and the video started with Brad clearing some brush from around the barn. Then there was some more video of him cleaning out junk and explaining that the barn would become the main dining hall of the church camp.

I really was into the video. It seems that Brad had a pretty grand vision for how he was going to transform his grandparent's former farm into a wonderful camp for the youth of his church. But Erin was curled up on the sofa next to me and had her head lying on my shoulder. I put my arm around her and she snuggled in even closer. I didn't want to move from this spot.

The video played for about an hour. Brad and I each had another drink, but the girls were both out cold. I didn't want to move Erin and wake her up; although I'm pretty sure she was passed out. Brad and I talked for a few more minutes and then his yawn indicated that it was time for us to go.

"I was serious earlier when I offered the BMW to you. You should take Erin for a ride tomorrow."

"That's a good idea. We'll see what time we get up and I'll come over if we decide to go for a ride."

I nudged Erin and said it was time to go. She mostly woke up, but not all the way. I put my arm around her and led her up the stairs. Brad and Kristy showed us out and we said we would talk tomorrow.

All the way up the driveway and across the front yard I had my arm around Erin and she had her head on my shoulder. We made it in the front door and I locked it behind us as I walked her down the hall to my room.

Erin asked if she could make a pit stop at the bathroom. I waited outside the bathroom door for her and then helped her toward the bed where she immediately fell on the mattress and pulled the pillow under her head. I slipped her shoes and glasses off of her and pulled the covers up over her shoulders and slipped into bed on the other side. I'd had quite a bit to drink myself and was having trouble keeping my eyes open, but I didn't want to sleep.

I wanted to lay there and watch her. She was so perfect. Her body has always been amazing, even as freshmen in high school, but seeing her now, as a full grown woman was overwhelming to me.

I wanted to put my arm around her; so I did. I wanted to pull my body close to hers; so I did. I wanted to listen to her breathe and smell her hair and run my hand across her hip and thigh; so I did.

My heart was pounding out of my chest. I'd been dreaming of this moment for eight years. The moment when Erin and I would first share a bed.

She let out a deep sigh and a slight moan. I nuzzled myself closer to her until the space between our bodies was gone. I gave her a gentle kiss on her neck and again I heard the faintest moan. I continued kissing her neck and shoulder while gently rubbing her hip and thigh. My pelvis was pressed up against the back of her body and as I continued kissing I began pressing my hips against hers.

My hand had crept further up her thigh and inside the hem of her shorts. Her skin was so smooth and soft. I wrapped my arm all the way around her and pulled her body even closer to mine. I put my hand under her shirt and rubbed her stomach, still kissing her neck and ear. As I moved my hand down to the button of her shorts she let out another moan, a little louder this time. She rolled to her back and mumbled something that sounded like, "Oh Luke. I love you sweetie, but not tonight. I promise, first thing in the morning."

I yanked my hand away and propped myself up on one elbow. Had I heard her right? Did she call me Luke? Who in the hell is Luke?

I didn't know what to do. My heart was beating faster now, but for a different reason. My ears were ringing and my face was flush. I felt like I'd been run over by a truck. All of a sudden I was no longer tired. I didn't touch her again the rest of the night, but I also didn't take my eyes off her. I was in love and furious and confused all at the same time.

It had to be a mistake. She's drunk and probably having a dream. Although I don't know what kind of dream would involve her being in bed with someone named Luke. I wasn't going to sleep and we were going to get to the bottom of this, first thing in the morning.

XXII

I sat awake all night. There were too many things going through my head to sleep. Multiple times I wanted to snuggle her again. I knew that she had to be drunk and confused when she called me Luke. I honestly considered the fact that I could probably get her completely undressed while she was out, but that I would probably regret it if I did. So I mostly just rehearsed in my head how the conversation would go in the morning.

"Are you aware that you called me Luke last night?"

"Um, uh, no. Are you sure? Are you sure I said Luke? I don't even know anyone named Luke. We were both pretty drunk. I must have been mumbling and you just didn't understand me."

Or

"So, Erin. Who's Luke?"

"Um, I don't know anyone named Luke. Why do you ask?"

"Oh no reason. You just called me Luke in your sleep last night and said that you would have sex with him first thing this morning. That's all. That's the only reason I'm asking. No big deal."

Or

"Erin, something has been bothering me all night. I barely slept because of it."

"Really, what's bothering you sweetheart?"

"Well, when we got home last night and were all snuggled up in bed; I thought I heard you call me Luke. You were mumbling a little, so I can't be entirely certain, but it sure did sound like you called me Luke."

"Oh honey, I can see how that would bother you. I was pretty drunk last night. I really don't even remember coming home. I honestly don't know anyone named Luke and if I called you that or something that sounded like that, I am so sorry. Get back in this bed with me and let's see if we can't make it all better."

I really don't think I had ever endured such a long night in my life. Finally, when I saw the first hint of light streaming in from outside, I got up and went to the kitchen to make breakfast. I still wasn't sure which approach I was going to take, but we were going to have the conversation about Luke.

XXIII

I got everything ready in the kitchen, but didn't cook yet. I figured I'd let Erin sleep as late as she wanted. Several times I went back to the bedroom and peaked in at her. Watching her sleep, bathed in the morning light, in my bed, just like I'd always wanted, calmed my anger from the night before.

Maybe it would be a good idea to start the morning on a positive note and not ask about Luke until a little later in the day.

I went back to the kitchen to make sure everything was perfect and didn't notice that Erin followed me from the room.

"Good morning Rob." She said, with the voice of an angel. Well maybe the voice of a hung-over angel with a frog in her throat.

"Good morning Erin. How do you feel this morning?"

"Surprisingly, not as bad as I thought I would. I don't remember the last time I had that much to drink."

"Me neither, I lied.

"How about some pancakes with fresh strawberries for breakfast?"

"Oh, that sounds good. Do you have any coffee ready?"

"Yep. Two sugars and a cream?"

"You know me well Rob Anderson."

"So, what did you think of the neighbors and the party last night?" I asked as I handed her a cup of coffee.

"Brad and Kristy are pretty amazing. And they have such a great story. Can you imagine? Two people who meet as freshmen in high school and after everything that they've been through and they're still together and, and really, they're living the American Dream. I have never in my life met anyone like them."

Once again Erin managed to completely dumbfound me. Have I ever heard of two people who met as freshman in high school and even after everything they have been through together, they are still together and living the American Dream? Hello, what about us?

Oh yeah, Erin managed to throw a wrench in our plans, but still, it's a minor set-back. The day will come with the grandkids playing in the backyard after Thanksgiving dinner. I have no doubt.

"Erin," I said as I flipped a pancake.

"Do you ever wonder what our future holds? Do you think it will turn out like we've always thought it would?"

"Well, honestly, I don't think a lot about the future. I mean I have goals and I think I know that I want to start my career as a prosecutor and then probably join a law firm once I have a little experience."

"That's not what I mean Erin. I mean do you think about our future together and if it will still be what we always wanted it to be?"

"I'm not sure I know what you're asking me Rob. I think we'll always be friends and probably always stay in touch."

"Erin, what are you talking about? Always be friends? Probably always stay in touch?

"I'm talking about *us* Erin and the eight year relationship that we've had. And the plans to go to undergrad at Mizzou and then you go to law school at Wash U and then I would go back and get my MBA and then we would get married and buy a house and start a family and some day when we're old and gray we would watch our grandkids playing in the yard after Thanksgiving dinner!"

"Rob! I'm pretty sure I never made those plans. I'm sorry that I didn't choose Wash U for law school, but honestly, MU was the best fit for me. This is my career and I'm not going to go just anywhere to law school. I had to make the decision that was best for me.

"And marriage and kids and buying a house and grandkids at Thanksgiving dinner? Rob, we've never even dated!"

I was seeing black spots again and I could feel my pulse in my ears. I tried to talk, but nothing would come out. I leaned forward and put my hands on the kitchen island to steady myself.

Erin jumped out of her seat and came around to my side of the island.

"Rob, the pancakes are burning," she said as she took them off the griddle and tossed them in the sink.

"Rob, I don't know how you ever got the idea that we were going to be together and be married. I apologize if my coming here this weekend somehow lead you to believe that we were more than just great friends.

"Rob, you have always been a great friend. From that first church barbeque back in Shelbyville, you were so polite and kind and I've always considered you a great friend. Almost like a brother. I'm sorry if you thought there was more to our friendship, but I don't think of you like that. I hope you can understand."

I didn't speak. I couldn't speak. I was having trouble catching my breath and I really thought that I might pass out.

"Rob, I'm going to go use the restroom. I'll give you a few minutes."

XXIV

I was trying to make sense of what I had just heard. It was like she was trying to tell me that the last eight years of my life never happened. I felt like I had just woken up from a deep sleep and a wonderful dream only to realize that it was all make believe.

But it wasn't. I didn't imagine meeting her at the church barbeque the summer before our freshman year in high school, she just said so herself. I didn't imagine spending time with her to develop the first FBLA club at Shelbyville high school; I have yearbook photos to prove it. I didn't imagine going to dozens of social events together throughout high school and college. I know for a fact that we studied together at least twice a week during most of our four years together at Mizzou.

I also know that we ended every semester by going to dinner together, just the two of us. I know that is a fact because it was during our second to last dinner that she first shattered the plans that we had spent seven years making.

I had to have answers.

I walked down the hallway toward the bedroom and peaked in the door. She was sitting on the edge of the bed, talking on her phone. She noticed me looking in the door.

"Okay, I've gotta go. I'll talk to you again in just a little bit. No, I'm fine. I promise, I'm fine. I'll see you soon."

"Who was that Erin?"

"That was a friend of mine from Columbia. Listen, Rob. I'm not sure how you got it in your head that we're a couple. We've never been a couple. We've always been great friends and that's all we'll ever be."

"Erin, you're wrong. I've been in love with you since the first time I met you and I know that you feel the same way about me. We've planned our entire lives together. We've been talking about our future together since we were fourteen!"

"Rob, when we used to get together and discuss how to set up and run the FBLA and how to prepare for state competitions; back when we were the only two members of the organization, we did discuss our futures, but I never intended that our futures would be together. You told me your plans and goals and dreams and I told you mine. That's how we became such close friends."

"Erin, I have done everything in my power to follow through on those plans and goals and dreams. I've made sacrifices so that we could follow the course that we laid out together eight years ago and now, all of a sudden, you're telling me that I mean nothing to you!"

"No. I never said that you don't mean anything to me. I said that we never made plans together. I'm sorry if you misinterpreted our conversations, but Rob, I never asked you to make any sacrifices for me."

"Erin, we had a plan! You are supposed to be at Wash U and you're supposed to be living in this house with me so we can grow closer and grow as a couple, just like we did last night at the party. If you had followed the plan we could have experiences like that every day and see the plan through."

"Rob, I still have goals and dreams, but plans change. Wash U wasn't a good fit for me. I'm sorry, but I have never made decisions about my future based on what your choices would be. I told you that you should explore every option available to you before taking a job. You never even looked outside of St. Louis."

"*That's because the plan was to go to St. Louis together!*" I yelled.

"Okay Rob, you're starting to scare me and I'm not going to be yelled at. Apparently there has been a huge misunderstanding of our friendship. I think it would be best if I head back to Columbia now."

"One question Erin, before you go."

"Yes Rob, what's that?"

"Who is Luke?"

XXV

Silence wasn't the answer I expected. I watched her face turn red. I could tell she was afraid to answer. I felt a strange sense of power and control over the situation, as if I had her on the ropes and she was about to break and tell me how sorry she was and confess her love for me. So I asked again.

"Who is Luke? You called me Luke last night in your sleep and I was just wondering if Luke is a real person."

"I called you Luke? When did I do that? Were you in bed with me?"

"Has Luke been in bed with you?"

"Rob, you don't have control of my personal life! And you are *not* welcome in my bed!"

"But you were in *my* bed! And you were getting turned on by me touching you and you called me Luke. Is Luke a real person? It's a straight-forward question Erin."

"Rob! I was drunk and I thought you were a better friend than that. I can't believe you got in bed with me when I was passed out. I was *not* getting turned on by you. You have completely violated my trust in you! What did you do to me?"

"Relax Erin. I rubbed your back and snuggled with you. I was pretty drunk myself. Nothing inappropriate happened."

"You getting in bed with me was inappropriate Rob."

"Erin, you never answered my question. Is Luke a real person?"

She exhaled deeply through her nose and looked away from me.

"Luke is a very dear friend of mine. We're very close."

"Is he your boyfriend?"

"Yes, I suppose you could say that. I think you reach a certain point in your life where the terms *boyfriend* and *girlfriend* are a little juvenile. Adult relationships can't really be characterized with the same verbiage as Junior High relationships."

"I don't understand what you're saying Erin. Are you and Luke in a relationship together or not?"

"Yes, Rob. Luke and I live together. I moved in with him last month. I've known him for almost a year. He's the reason that I decided to stay in Columbia for law school. He's an attorney at a law firm in Jefferson City. I am very much in love with him. Is that what you wanted to hear?"

I let out a slight laugh that sounded more like a grunt. I couldn't talk. I was having trouble breathing and it felt like my throat was closing and I swallowed hard just to get a breath. I turned my gaze away from her and grunted again. I felt dizzy and I couldn't see through the tears welling up in my eyes. But I had to know more. I had to know how long she had been deceiving me. I had to know if the purity of my angel was tarnished.

"You, you, you *live* together? Like you live together under the same roof? In the same house?"

"Well, he actually has an apartment. It's not a house, but, yes, we both live under the same roof."

"How many bedrooms does this apartment have?"

She wrinkled her nose and sat up straight on the edge of the bed. She looked right at me with a very confused, condescending look.

"How many bedrooms? Why in the world does that matter? It has two. If that's really important."

I was choking back the vomit and the tears and the urge to pass out. Maybe, just maybe, they were very good friends who happened to share living space. After all, the apartment did have two bedrooms.

"So you each have your own room?"

"Rob! You need to grow up and get a grip on reality. Luke is my 'boyfriend', she said as she made little quotation marks with her fingers.

"We live together because we are in love. I can honestly say that I can see myself spending the rest of my life with him. Our apartment...it has two bedrooms, but one of them is an office! We share a bedroom. We share a bed. We are a couple and we have been for quite some time. What part of this is still confusing to you?"

I had to hear it from her. I couldn't make assumptions. I was fighting back tears and I was having trouble breathing and my face was bright red and my ears were ringing and I didn't know if I would actually live through the answer to the next question, but I had to ask it.

"So.

Deep breath and deep exhale.

"You share a bedroom and a bed.

I swallowed hard and looked away.

"Does that mean that you have slept with him? I mean,

obviously, you have both slept together in the same bed, so of course you have slept *with* him, but have you…have you had sex with him? Does your relationship involve sexual intercourse? That's what I need to know."

"Rob! You don't need to know that. It's none of your business. I'm a grown woman who lives with her significant other. Grow the hell up and figure it out for yourself!"

"No! I want you to say it. I want you to tell me. I want you to tell me that you've become a slut and that saving yourself for marriage and saving yourself for me no longer means anything to you!"

"Rob! You're insane. I'm leaving right now! I don't even know who you are. This is ridiculous. I don't owe you an explanation for my relationship with Luke."

"Say it! Say it Erin! Tell me that you and Luke have sex!!!!!" I screamed.

"Of course we have sex. Is that what you want to know? Is that what is going to make you happy and allow you to move forward with your life? Rob, I am in love with Luke. And, if he asks me, I will marry him."

All of a sudden, I was calm. My breathing was still very deep and deliberate, but the rest of my anxiety symptoms were gone.

"Erin. We used to sit together in your father's teen Sunday school classes and discuss human sexuality and procreation and marriage and family. Your father made it very clear that sexual relations are reserved exclusively for marriage.

"You and I even had discussions outside of Sunday school class. We talked about the importance of saving ourselves for marriage. We talked about the importance of saving ourselves for each other. It was all part of the plan."

"Rob, some of us still act like we're 15 years old…and some of us grew up. I am done talking about my love life with you. I really think I'm ready to leave now. I don't want to talk anymore about this."

"Did you give your virginity to Luke?"

"Rob! I said I'm done. I'm not answering anymore of your inappropriate questions."

"It's a simple question Erin. Is Luke the first guy you ever slept with?"

"Rob, I have always felt a little bit sorry for you. You've always had a hard time fitting in. That's why I allowed you to get close to me. I thought I was doing what my father asked during Sunday school. I was accepting the outsiders, just like Jesus would have done. I tried to include you in everything that happened in high school. I tried to include you in social life in college. I cared for you, like a brother.

She was crying now and her body was trembling. Her voice was shaking as she tried to finish her thought. Through tears and snot and a shaky voice, I think I heard her say,

"All I ever wanted to do was see you be happy and find a place to fit in. I never thought that you would mistake it for feelings of love."

But I was calm now. The anxiety had passed.

"Erin, you never answered the question. Is Luke the first guy you ever slept with?"

"Do you really want to know? If that was the last question you could ever ask me; if my reply is the last words you will ever hear from my voice; is that what you really want to know?"

"Yes."

"Okay. Just remember that you asked. And just remember that these are the last words you will ever hear me speak."

"I have to know."

"Rob. I dated Steve Everton for nearly three years in high school. I don't know how you could not have known that! We were homecoming king and queen. We were prom king and queen. We were a couple. He tried to give me a promise ring for Christmas our senior year. I couldn't accept it because I knew there was no way that I would ever marry him. But, during Christmas break, do you remember the night that practically the entire school went down to the Shelbina City Lake? We were all riding four-wheelers and sledding and playing on the frozen lake. Do you remember that night?"

"Yes. I remember. I had a lot to drink that night."

"Yes, you did. You having a lot to drink seemed to be a reoccurring theme of our senior year in high school, and just like each time before and each time after that night, I asked David to take you home because you were drunk and I knew that David was a good friend to you and that he would make sure you got home safe. And you did. But the rest of us stayed out at the lake for several more hours. And before I went home that night...I lost my virginity to Steve.

"And I knew that I would never marry him, and I knew that as soon as high school was over, our relationship would end!

"Is that really what you wanted to know Rob? Do you want to know about the guys I dated in college too? There's more than one! But less than four! Does that make me a slut, Rob?

"Rob, ask yourself this, who's the normal one here?"

The wind was rushing back through my ears. The room was spinning and my throat was closing. I tried to swallow, but it was so dry that it made me gag. My entire life plan didn't just have a wrench in it, it was destroyed. In my mind, at that moment, there was no plan B. There was no way to recover from this moment.

XXVI

"Rob, I'm really not sure if our friendship can recover from this. Don't call or text me. Maybe, someday, in the future, we can be friends again. But certainly not right now. Goodbye Rob."

And with that, she walked out of the bedroom that we had just shared the night before, and down the hallway and through the laundry room and out of the garage. She got in her car and backed out of the driveway that should have been ours together for the next year…and drove away.

Everything that I had known to be alive was dead. Everything that I had ever known to be real was fake. Everything that I had trusted to be true was false. I collapsed on the bed and sobbed.

I'm not sure how long I lay there. I tried to replay the past 12 hours in my mind. I tried to recreate the moment that my life disintegrated, but the story kept pausing on the moment she called me Luke.

Could I have done something different? Should I have said something else? For God's sake, she slept with Steve Everton in high school! Maybe I should have done things differently years ago. Was there a defining moment? Was there a moment when she was mine and I lost her?

I tried to replay years of experiences together over and over in my head, but I just couldn't concentrate. Maybe she was right? Maybe I'm not normal. I'm only what I know how to be…and that is madly in love with Erin McMillen. I could continue to lay here on the bed and feel sorry for myself and cry like a schoolboy, or I could stand up like a man, draw my sword and go get her back.

Brad's words from the night before came back to me. Erin *was* someone I would lay down my life for and I would fight anyone who stood in the way of our happiness. I would prove to her that I was the man she needed in her life. I got up off the bed, wiped my tears and chose the latter.

XXVII

I've always been a rational, logical guy. I've always thought things out and anticipated the outcomes of each path available to me. It really is what set me apart from my peers at an early age, everyone said so.

I couldn't just go running off to Columbia and show up at her doorstep with a dozen roses and expect her to jump in the car with me and come back to Ladue. No, it was going to take a little convincing, but the convincing needed to be done on my turf.

One way or the other, I needed to get her back here, under my roof, so I could prove to her what an amazing life we would have together if she would just give it a chance. So, I was going to have to take a calculated risk, something that I didn't do very often, and hope that in the end it would be the right action to take.

I really had no intention of harming this Luke guy. Hell, I didn't even know him well enough to hate him. I knew Steve Everton, and I had hated him for a long time, and I really couldn't see myself harming Steve. Unless, of course, Steve was harming me or someone I cared about, then I could probably bring myself to kill him if necessary. Of course, it wouldn't be my choice, it would be his.

And so I rationalized my thoughts about Luke. It wouldn't be my choice, it would be his. My Uncle Rich had told me all about Ambassador Nichols' gun collection and since I hadn't seen it anywhere in the house, I had to assume that it was locked up in his private study. I had no key and I had no locksmith expertise, but with a few hard kicks I was able to kick the door in.

I really wasn't concerned about the broken door at that point, but in the back of my head I told myself that I would have plenty of time in the future to get it fixed before Ambassador Nichols would see it. The fact that I could still rationalize fixing a broken door jamb at a later date told me that I wasn't crazy. I was thinking very clearly at the moment and I knew exactly what I was going to do and exactly what the outcome would be.

I found the guns and carefully chose an older looking Colt .357 and a box of ammo. I really hoped that I wouldn't need any ammo, but again, that would be Luke's choice, not mine. I reassured myself that this was a rational, logical decision. After all, I had chosen an older gun that would be less likely to be able to be traced and it was a large caliber, so it would only take one shot; if that's what Luke chose.

I found some zip-ties and duct tape in the garage. As much as I wanted Erin to come back with me of her own free will, I figured that that probably wouldn't happen. My efforts at winning her back would have to be after we were already back here, under *our* roof. So, I had to be prepared to bring her back against her will, although as gently as possible.

I calmly walked over to Brad's house and knocked on the front door. I didn't even know what time it was, but it seemed to take him an eternity to answer the door.

"Hey Brad, I recall last night that you offered your Beemer for Erin and me to go for a cruise…"

"Absolutely! Let me grab the keys and I'll meet you around back by the garage." He said through sleepy eyes and a gravelly voice.

I walked down the driveway just as the garage door was opening. There was Brad to meet me.

"Here you go. Have a great time. And don't worry about

putting any gas in it before you bring it back. This one's on me."

"Thanks Brad, I really appreciate it. I'll take good care of it."

I tossed my duffle bag of supplies in the passenger seat and backed out of Brad's garage. I shifted into first and then to second before I hit the end of the driveway and turned left to head toward the interstate. Erin had a 20 minute lead on me, but I knew I should be able to catch her before she got to Columbia and she would lead me right to her and Luke's love shack.

XXVIII

"Was that Rob borrowing the car?" asked Kristy.

"Yep. I hope they have a great time together. They seem like such a great couple and Rob is so in love with her. He's head over heels."

"About that. When I got up to get a cup of coffee about half an hour ago, I saw Erin pulling out of the driveway. Was she with him?"

"No. It was just Rob. Maybe she ran an errand earlier and he came to get the car and just now went back to the house to pick her up."

"Brad, he just turned out of the driveway and sped away. He didn't stop back at his house."

"Well, who knows? Maybe she's leaving her car somewhere and he's going to pick her up? Honey, I offered the car to him so he could take his girlfriend out for a cruise and a nice lunch and he took me up on the offer. I'm not going to worry too much about it."

"Brad, I'm not trying to say that there's anything fishy going on, but I do know that she's not really his girlfriend."

"Well they looked pretty cozy last night and Rob told me that they've been dating since they were in high school."

"Erin told me that they've been good friends since high school and that she's always thought of Rob like a brother. They have never dated. In fact, Erin lives with her boyfriend in Columbia. She just came down to visit Rob for the night because he really wanted a friend to go to the party with him.

"If you're not worried about it then I won't worry about it, but we're getting two different sides of the story. Erin also mentioned that Rob had some social anxiety issues and had been on medication for it since he was kid. She described him as just being socially awkward."

"I can see how he might be a little socially awkward, but he seemed fine just now. I'm not going to worry too much about it, but maybe I'll go over and talk to him later this evening."

XXIX

I was running just over 80 miles per hour down I-70. I was a little concerned about a traffic stop because that would ruin my entire plan. There was no way I would catch her and find out where she lived if I got stopped in a car that wasn't mine. I didn't even have Brad's phone number to call him if I did get stopped. However, if I didn't catch up with her I would never be able to find out where she lived.

I had a bit of a concern that they might live in a gated community and I wouldn't be able to get in past the gate. That wouldn't ruin the plan, but would certainly cause a bit of a problem. I didn't worry too much about the gate, after all, I was driving a BMW, and surely someone would let me in a fancy, gated community.

My mother tried to call. I really didn't have the time or the desire to talk to her right now. I was rehearsing in my head exactly how this would go. I was really hoping that I wouldn't have to use the gun. That was my last resort; and of course, Luke's choice, not mine.

I also had some concern about going to work tomorrow and leaving Erin alone at the house. That was a bridge I would cross tomorrow morning. Maybe a full afternoon and evening of just the two of us talking things out would be sufficient so that I wouldn't have to leave her tied up and gagged all day while I was at work. I knew there was a possibility that it could take a few days for her to come around to seeing things my way, but I just really hated the thought of leaving her like that during the day.

Maybe I would just call in sick. I hated to do that on my first day, but surely they wouldn't fire me for it, would they? After all, people do get sick from time to time. I can't help it that my sick day just happens to be on my first day of work.

About the time I passed Kingdom City my mom tried to call again. That concerned me a little bit. Twice in one hour, on a Sunday morning when she should be visiting with the McMillen's after church, and she's trying to call me? It made me wonder if Erin called her parents, or my parents, and told them that our weekend together didn't go as planned.

Oh well, I had plenty of time on the drive home, once everything was back to normal, to give her a call. I had important things to concentrate on right now.

I started doing the math in my head. Erin had a 20 minute head start and I know she doesn't speed; not even one mile over the speed limit. It was 105 miles from my door to the city limits of Columbia and if she was going 70 mph, which I know she was, it would take her exactly an hour and a half to get to the city limits.

I had to catch her before the city limits because I had no idea which exit she would take. I was driving about 85 mph and at that speed it would take me 78 minutes to the city limits. I wasn't going to make it! I was going to lose her before I caught her. I had to drive faster.

As soon as I hit the gas and passed a semi, I saw it. The red Pontiac with license plate number 1RA 503. I had that license plate memorized two years ago. I could recite it in my sleep. It had my initials on it for God sake!

I remember when she renewed her plates and I saw them for the first time. I knew it was a sign. I mentioned it to Erin and she just smiled and said "That's a pretty funny coincidence."

She didn't see the signs like I did. They were all around us. Everything I saw pointed to the fact that we were meant for each other. We were supposed to be together. She was doing everything she could to try and ruin her life, but I wasn't going to sit idly by and allow God's plan to be destroyed.

God put the wheels in motion eight years ago when he called Rev. McMillen to shepherd his flock in Shelbyville. That was the calling that brought us together. That was the calling that I now have to see through to completion.

XXX

I backed off a little bit. I really didn't think she would recognize the car, but I didn't want to be suspicious either. I left a few cars in-between us and watched her take the Highway 63 exit about a half mile ahead of me. She stayed in the left lane of the exit ramp and had her left blinker on.

I slowed down and made sure she was through the light before I crept up the ramp. I watched her head south on 63 and I fell into a line of traffic a little ways back. A few miles down the road she turned on her right blinker and headed for the AC exit. I knew that they would live on the south side of town. Even if I hadn't been following her, I probably could have narrowed down where they lived to three or four apartment complexes. I probably could have even found her car if I drove around the parking lots enough. I just wouldn't be able to know which apartment was theirs.

A few miles down AC she turned right onto Green Meadows Rd. She was heading for Deer Valley Apartments. Of course, only the best apartment complex in Columbia. I was still a few hundred yards behind her and I really hoped that she hadn't noticed the silver BMW following her since I-70. I never got close enough to see if she was on the phone or checking her rear-view mirror. I just had to assume that I was undetected.

I turned into the complex about 30 seconds after her and was afraid that I had lost her. I slowly made my way through the parking lot and caught her car on the other side out of the corner of my eye. I immediately pulled into a parking spot and watched her exit her car and walk up the sidewalk. She entered the unit on the lower level on the south side.

I took a deep breath. It was now or never Rob Anderson. It's too late to chicken out. I went over the plan in my head. I was going to have to carry the gun, but I would only actually use it if Luke forced me. The plan was fairly straight forward and fool-proof. Nothing elaborate. Go in, tell Luke this is how it's going to be and take Erin with me. I didn't want to bind her and force her at gun point, but I would if I had to.

I looked again in the rear-view mirror. There was no way she saw me following. It's go time!

XXXI

I got out of the car and started walking toward their apartment. All of a sudden it dawned on me that there was a possibility that Erin might not come with me quietly. She probably would, but there was always the possibility.

If she didn't come quietly, it would be very difficult to lead her 100 yards across a parking lot to where I was parked. I was going to have to pull right up to the front door and go in and get her.

I went back to the Beemer and drove around to her side of the parking area. I pulled right up next to her car and the sidewalk we would walk down. There was no way to hide now. If their blinds had been open she would have seen me park the car and get out. My element of surprise would be blown. I had to move quickly now.

I went over the plan one more time in my head. It was very well thought out and as long as everyone cooperated, it would result in no one getting hurt; except maybe Luke's feelings when Erin calls him tomorrow night to tell him that she's staying in St. Louis forever!

I slung the duffel bag over my left shoulder and stuck the revolver in the waistband of my pants. I opened the car door and looked around. I even surprised myself by how calm I was. This certainly wasn't part of my plan eight years ago, but it was a hell of a plan right now and it was going to work.

I shut the car door and started up the sidewalk.

XXXII

I stood in front of their door. There was no turning back. I'd come this far and I had to see the plan through to the end if I ever had any hope of being with Erin again.

I assumed that this Luke guy would answer the door, but I had a back-up plan in case it was Erin. I knocked on the door.

I waited for what seemed like five minutes, careful that I was off to the side and couldn't be seen through the peephole. I started to knock again when I heard the tumbler of the deadbolt turn. I reached for the grip of the pistol as the door opened.

The door swung wide open, which I wasn't expecting. I thought it would open slightly and I would immediately throw my shoulder into it knocking Luke back at the same time that I drew the gun, and I would have the upper hand as he stumbled backward and I entered the apartment in complete control of the situation.

But the door swung wide open and there stood Luke, looking at me confused.

"Can I help you?" He said.

I didn't know what to say. I didn't know what to do. This wasn't part of the plan.

"Can I help you?" He repeated.

I heard Erin's voice from the kitchen and a cabinet door close and footsteps walking across the kitchen floor and toward the doorway where she would be able to see who was at the door in about a half a second.

"Who is it honey?" She said.

For a brief second I wanted to turn and run. This had all been a huge mistake. What the hell was I thinking?

It was too late. Erin rounded the corner and saw me.

"Rob! What in the hell are you doing here! I told you that it would be a long time before I ever wanted to see you or speak to you again!"

One part of my brain was registering what she was saying, but I wasn't really listening. I still had my hand on the grip of the gun, just under my un-tucked shirt and in the waistband of my pants.

I pulled the gun and raised my arm. My elbow was bent about 90 degrees and my hand was near my chest. They could see that I had a gun, but I wasn't sure what I was supposed to do with it. Erin screamed. Her scream was mad, sad, angry, terrified all at the same time. I couldn't quite tell how she was feeling at that moment.

Luke realized who I was and started to say something.

"Look buddy. I'm not sure what you're doing, but you're not welcome here right now."

He started to push the door shut as Erin screamed again. Screaming was not part of my plan. Leave it to Erin to screw up my perfect plan once again.

Luke was closing the door in my face and when it was about five inches short of closed I remembered my original plan. I threw my shoulder against the door, but there was nothing holding it on the other side. I thought there would be some resistance, but it flung back open and my momentum carried me through the door jamb and, catching my foot on the sill, I went headfirst into the entry way and landed on the cold, hard tile of the foyer.

Luckily, I didn't drop the gun and as Luke was reaching down for me; possibly to help me up, or possibly to beat the shit out of me; I got to my feet and pointed the gun directly at his face.

Erin was still in the doorway to the kitchen and was talking very loudly. I don't know what she was saying because I was concentrating on Luke's face. He was definitely scared. This was the way the plan was supposed to go. Suddenly, I was calm again and thinking clearly.

I took my right foot and pushed the door closed.

"Erin, you're making me a little bit nervous. You need to calm down and be quiet," I said.

"No Rob! I do not need to be quiet! How dare you come into my home…"

"Erin, just calm down for a second and let's see what Rob has to say," said Luke, trying to act calm and mask the fear that I saw in his eyes.

"Rob, you have two minutes to explain yourself or I'm calling the police. You have really flipped this time. How dare you bring a gun into my house?"

"Erin, I think it's best if we just be quiet and listen for minute, okay sweetie?"

Luke was more cooperative than I had thought he would be, but as much as I had hoped he would be. I really didn't expect Erin to react the way she was, but I could deal with her in a moment. Right now the conversation was between Luke and me.

Luke had his right arm extended toward Erin and his hand was up, as if to tell her to stay where she was. His eyes never left mine. I could see the fear and I knew that I was in control of the situation, just like I had planned.

"So, Rob. What can we do for you today?"

Luke was trying his hardest to remain composed. Erin was sobbing lightly and breathing heavily. I wondered if anyone had heard her scream and might come to investigate.

I reached over and locked the deadbolt on the door. Erin gasped and sobbed a little harder. Luke motioned toward her with his hand and whispered, "Shh, shh, shh."

"This is a nice place you have here Luke."

"Thank you Rob."

"Of course, you should see my place in Ladue. It's the kind of castle that Erin deserves." I had rehearsed that line as part of my plan and smiled a little when I said it.

"I hear it's a nice place Rob. Congratulations on living there. Can I ask why you're here?"

"Sure. I'll tell you why I'm here. Why don't you go have a seat on the couch Luke? Erin, why don't you sit in that chair over there," I said, motioning with the barrel of my gun toward a large brown chair in the corner.

I could stand in one spot and see both of them in front of me. Luke hadn't taken his eyes off of me. Erin was looking back and forth between Luke and me.

"Let me tell you why I'm here, and if everyone cooperates, I won't be here long and everyone will live happily ever after."

XXXIII

"Luke, I'm not sure what Erin has told you about me, if anything. I'm sure she must have told you something before she came to visit me yesterday."

"She told me that you were among her first friends when her family moved to Shelbyville and that she thought of you like a brother."

"Uh huh. Right. Well, you see Luke, Erin and I had a wonderful evening last night. It was the kind of evening that I've dreamed about for eight years. It was perfect and it ended with the two of us in bed together. Did she tell you about that?"

"She mentioned something about having a great evening with her dear friend and both of you drinking too much and passing out and then she said that this morning you were a different person. She said you scared her a little bit and she decided it was time to come home. We were just discussing the details when you knocked on the door."

"Erin has nothing to be scared of. You on the other hand, you should be scared. Do you know what can happen to guys who interfere in someone's relationship?

"Listen Luke, Erin is a beautiful woman. Eight years ago she was a beautiful girl. She has had to endure guys hitting on her constantly since she was young. First it was the meathead jocks back in Shelbyville, then it was the douche-bag frat boys in college and now it seems to be the sleazy lawyers.

"I'm the only gentleman who has ever loved Erin. I'm the only man who treated her with the respect that she deserves. I'm the only one who has been there since day one. The only one not trying to get in her pants."

"What were you trying to do to me last night Rob? You never have explained exactly what happened after I passed out."

"Erin, I already told you that nothing inappropriate happened. I was a gentleman. I hugged you and caressed you the way a gentleman would. Do you think Luke would have stopped just because you were passed out?"

"Rob, I still don't understand why you're here. Yes, Erin is a beautiful woman and I agree that she needs to be treated well and I do that the best I can. I don't really seem to get any complaints from her.

"I'm sorry that things didn't work out between the two of you. It sounds like maybe one of you had feelings that the other didn't have. Maybe it was just a matter of me being in the right place at the right time. You know, the right timing has a lot to do with it.

"But, I do love Erin very much and I can promise you that I will take very good care of her. If you love her as much as you say you do, then you should want her to be happy, not terrified."

I smiled a little bit. Erin isn't terrified of me. She does love me. Love isn't supposed to be easy. The raw emotion that we both felt this morning, that's the emotion of love. A couple that has never had a disagreement can't really be in love. Love requires that both partners are open and honest about their feelings, even if those feelings occasionally hurt their partner. It's better to be honest than to keep it bottled up inside. Erin and I were honest with each other this morning. It was a small lover's quarrel and now it was time to go home and make up. Time for phase two of my plan.

XXXIV

"Both of you, head into the bedroom," I said as I motioned with the barrel of the gun.

"Rob, please don't do anything that you'll regret," pleaded Erin.

"Just cooperate and no one will get hurt. That much I promise you."

I entered the bedroom behind them. I was really hoping that the bed would have a headboard with spindles, that would make the plan much easier, but I had thought ahead and had a backup plan.

"Luke, lay down in the center of the bed."

"Rob, what are you going to do to him? Please, don't hurt anyone."

"I told you that if everyone cooperates then no one will get hurt. I want this to be over as quickly as possible so I can leave. Now Luke, lie down in the center of the bed on your back."

Luke laid down on the bed and Erin's sobs started back up again. I took the duffel bag and threw it on the end of the bed.

"Erin, open the bag and get the zip-ties out."

"Rob, please don't do this. Please don't make me hurt him. Maybe we can go back in the living room and the three of us can talk through this."

"Erin, this is the third time I've told you. If everyone cooperates then no one will get hurt. I don't plan on hurting Luke and I'm not going to ask you to hurt him. I just want you to get the zip-ties out of the bag."

Erin unzipped the bag and started taking the items out. Duct tape, box of ammo, zip-ties.

Holy shit! The ammo! I had never even loaded the gun. Here I was trying to be a Barney bad-ass and my gun has been unloaded the whole time. What in the hell am I going to do? Luke is physically bigger and stronger than me. It wouldn't take much for him to beat the snot out of me. Hell, he might even have a gun of his own in the night stand. If he knows that my gun isn't loaded, he could grab his and shoot me. And, he'd be completely justified in doing so. I couldn't let on that my sword was no more dangerous than a wet noodle.

Erin was looking at me, holding the zip-ties, still sobbing lightly. Luke was lying on the bed like I had asked him to. I had to think quickly.

"Erin, I would like for you to put one zip-tie around each of Luke's wrists and each of his ankles. Make them fairly tight. But not so tight that they cut off his circulation. Remember, I'm not here to hurt anyone."

As Erin moved toward Luke on the bed, I grabbed the items and put them back in the duffel bag. I'm pretty sure it didn't register with either of them that the gun might not even be loaded. If it had, Erin wouldn't be putting zip-ties on Luke right now. From now on, the duffel bag stays with me. Hopefully we can speed this along and me, Erin and my wet noodle can be on the road in about 10 minutes.

She had a zip-tie on each wrist and each ankle.

"Now use another one to connect the wrists together and then the ankles together."

I was looking around the room trying to figure out what his zip-tie restraints were going to be attached to. There was a small chair, a couple of night stands, two large dressers. There just didn't seem to be anything that would make sense.

Erin had connected the wrists and the ankles and was looking at me again. I glanced down and saw the feet of the footboard. That would work perfect! But now his wrists were bound together and I wanted them separate; one wrist and one ankle in each corner of the bed.

Oh well, I was already nervous about the bullet-less gun and I didn't want them to think that I didn't know what I was doing.

"Erin, put a zip-tie around the leg on the footboard and one on the headboard. Then make a length of zip-ties to connect the wrists to the headboard and the ankles to the footboard."

As Erin walked toward the headboard she stopped near Luke's head. She placed her hand on his cheek and whispered, "I'm so sorry." Then she bent forward and kissed him gently. I could handle one last good-bye kiss, even though I didn't like it.

The wrists were attached to the headboard and the ankles to the footboard. I tugged on the zip-ties to make sure they were tight. I didn't see any way that Luke was going to be able to get loose by himself. I reached in the duffel bag and got the tape.

"I really don't want to do this Luke, but I can't take any chances. Erin, put a piece of Duct tape over his mouth."

"Rob, please! He's not going anywhere."

"It's not about going anywhere. It's about making noise. I'll even let you cut a slit in the tape so it's easier for him to breathe."

"Just put it on honey. Everything is going to be fine. Just put the tape over my mouth."

Erin placed a piece of tape over Luke's mouth and I pressed it down to make sure it stuck.

"Erin, can you go and get yours and Luke's cell phones please?"

Erin walked out of the bedroom toward the kitchen and it hit me that she could make a run for the door. I was getting lazy and it was going to cost me. Luke wasn't going anywhere so I quickly followed Erin to the kitchen. She started to pick up both phones from the kitchen counter and I stepped in front of her and grabbed them.

"Sorry, sweetie. I better hold these. It's not that I don't trust you, it's just that I have a plan and you know that I like to be in control of my plans."

"Yes Rob, I know." Her face was swollen and her eyes were red. I had never seen her look so horrible in my life. You would think I had just run over her puppy the way she was reacting.

"Let's head back to the bedroom please."

"Whatever I have to do to cooperate Rob."

XXXV

"Erin, I'd like you to pack a bag with the things you'll need."

"What things Rob?"

"Just pack the things you'll need for an extended stay. Phone charger, make-up, pajamas, and a few changes of clothes. Maybe something nice to wear, like you were going out on the town."

"Rob, I'm not leaving here with you."

"But, you are Erin. That's the next step in the plan. I can't very well carry out the rest of the plan in this apartment."

"Rob, whatever you have planned, it's not going to work and it's going to end very badly for you. I'm not leaving this apartment with you."

"Erin, I have been telling you all along that if everyone cooperates, then no one will get hurt. So far, everyone has cooperated and everyone is still fine; even if someone is a little tied up at the moment."

"So what are you going to do Rob? If I don't leave with you then you're going to shoot me? How does that help you accomplish whatever this plan of yours is?"

"No Erin. I'm not going to shoot you. I'm going to shoot him and then I'm going to bind and tape you and carry you out of here. I don't want to do it that way, but you already messed up one of my plans and I'll be damned if I let you do it again."

"Rob, you are not going to shoot Luke. That's not who you are. You are logical and rational, remember? That's what you've always told me."

"Well I'm not going to shoot him right away. I was hoping you would just cooperate and we could walk out the door, but…" I walked over to Luke and with the butt of the gun I smacked him on the bridge of his nose.

I really didn't think I hit him that hard. I just wanted to show Erin that I meant business. Behind the tape I could hear Luke's muffled moans of pain. Blood was streaming out of both nostrils and he had a gash across his nose. The sight of the blood was horrendous and I thought he might choke on it. I knew he was swallowing blood and with the tape on he couldn't spit it out. Shit, he was going to gag on his own blood. I started to panic and quickly pulled the tape back and a mouth full of blood was spit all over the bed.

"Oh my God, Rob! What in the hell are you doing? You're going to kill him. Let me untie him right now."

"Stay right there Erin," I said, holding the gun over his nose again.

Luke was still sputtering and coughing and gagging on blood and the flow from his nose wasn't slowing down. The sight of blood pooling around his head and neck was actually quite gruesome and I had to turn away to keep from gagging myself.

I looked at Erin and tried to compose myself.

"Erin, I didn't want to have to do that. I asked you to pack a bag and come with me. As long as you cooperate, there will be no more pain for anyone."

"Erin, go ahead and pack a bag. I'm fine. Just do what he says."

It felt good to be in control of the situation, but I did feel a little bit sorry for Luke. I felt that it would be appropriate to show Erin my compassionate side.

"If you would like, you can also get Luke a cold wash-rag for his face. He's kind of making a mess on his bed"

XXXVI

Erin had her bag packed and was standing in the doorway of the master bathroom looking at Luke and sobbing.

"Do you have everything you need dear?"

Her stone-faced glare in my direction indicated that she probably had everything she would need. The blood was no longer gushing from Luke's nose, although he was quite a mess. I got a fresh piece of Duct tape and placed it back over his mouth.

"Erin, it really is time to go. Everything will be fine, you'll see."

She didn't budge, so I walked over to her and put my hand on her arm to guide her out the door. She twisted away from me and started walking toward the bedroom door. As she walked past the dresser she stopped to pick up her cell phone.

"I'll take that," I said and threw it in the duffel bag.

I hadn't originally thought about Luke's cell phone. It was one of the very few details I had overlooked in the plan. His phone was still on the dresser, next to where Erin had just picked up hers. As we walked toward the bedroom door to leave, I took the butt of the gun and smashed his phone, just as I had done to his nose about 10 minutes ago.

Erin was standing in the door looking over her shoulder at Luke and crying. She mouthed *"I love you."* Luke did his best to nod his head. Poor guy, goodbyes are hard enough when you're not tied to a bed and laying in a pool of your own blood and snot. Oh well, he'll be fine. After all, he's an attorney and I'm sure there's no shortage of girls waiting to throw themselves at his feet. Just not mine.

XXXVII

Erin and I paused by the front door.

"Are you sure you have everything you're going to need?" I said as she glared at me again.

"You know what we might want Erin? How about if we get yours and Luke's keys. I think that's the last thing we'll need."

She walked to the kitchen and came back with two sets of keys.

"Perfect. I think we're all ready to head out. You know Erin, I know you're a little confused and probably a little scared, but everything is going to work out just fine. We're going to be happy together. You'll see. Someday, 50 years from now, we'll look out the window after Thanksgiving dinner and watch the grandkids playing in the yard and we'll put our arms around each other and smile."

"Screw you Rob," was her reply.

"Now Erin, before we walk out this door, I have to be able to trust you. I don't want to have to tie you up or put tape on your mouth, but I have to know that you're not going to run or scream. We're just going to quietly walk to the car and get in and drive away."

"And what if I don't cooperate?"

"If you don't cooperate then a bloody nose is going to be the least of Luke's problems."

Erin opened the front door and mumbled, "Let's go."

I placed the gun back in my pants and covered it with my shirt. I pulled the door shut behind us and found a key to lock the deadbolt.

We got in the car and backed out of the parking spot. I made sure to lock the car doors and put the child safety lock on. I put the gun on the floor board by my feet and we were on our way *home*.

XXXVIII

I hadn't really given much thought to the conversation that we would have on the drive home. It was another oversight in my plan. Erin not only wasn't talking, she also wasn't looking at me. In fact, she looked kind of pissed.

"Are you hungry sweetie? Do you want to stop and get a drink or something to eat?"

She mumbled something in reply.

"What's that dear?"

"No Rob! I'm not hungry and I don't want something to eat! What I want to know is what in the hell are you thinking? Do you really think this is going to have a happy ending?"

I wasn't prepared to have this discussion on the drive home. I had our discussion planned, but it needed to take place back at the house. We really needed to be in a luxurious surrounding for the words that I had planned to have the most affect.

"Erin, as I said before, I know you're confused and scared, but this will all make perfect sense. Just wait until we get home. I love you sweetie."

"Screw you Rob. You're going to go to jail, you know that don't you? You're going to go away for a very long time. Do you want me to start listing the charges that will be against you? Assault, kidnapping, brandishing a firearm, breaking and entering,…"

"I did not break and enter! Luke opened the door for me. I knocked and he opened the door. I'm not the one who tied Luke up, you did that. I didn't kidnap you. The apartment security cameras will show that you and I walked out together, you were under your own freewill. I had even put the gun away by then. Maybe, just maybe, I assaulted Luke, but I didn't mean to hit him that hard, I promise. Really Erin, you have to believe me, I didn't intend to hit him that hard. And I'll apologize the next time I see him. Heck, we can even invite him to our wedding."

"Rob, you are completely delusional. You are going to prison. Have you given any consideration to how you're going to survive prison? That's where the bad guys go. The guys in there, they'll beat you and rape you and they'll laugh about it. They have no conscious. They won't gag and turn away at the sight of a broken nose like you did."

"Erin, I really think that if we just reflect on the good times that we've had together, including the party last night and really think about how happy we were together during those times, and quit focusing on the negative, this ride is going to be much more enjoyable and it will be easier to transition into phase three of the plan when we get home."

"You belong in a mental hospital Rob, you really do."

The rest of the ride home was quiet and it gave me time to rehearse the events for the remainder of the day. It would be early afternoon when we returned, just like I had planned. The rest of the day was going to be phenomenal and was going to be the beginning of the rest of our phenomenal lives together.

I rolled down my window and tossed hers and Luke's keys out the window into the median of the interstate. This was truly the start of a new life for Erin and me.

XXXIX

We were driving down the street toward the house when it occurred to me that I needed to return the car to Brad. I hadn't really thought about how I was going to do that. Erin had been fairly cooperative up until this point in the plan, but I just didn't think that I could risk putting her in front of Brad and Kristy right now. Besides, she really didn't look very good at the moment. The crying had stopped a while ago, but she kind of looked like maybe she was still a little hung over from last night.

I decided that I would pull in our driveway, use the garage door opener and get her in the house and settled and then take the car back over to Brad. We pulled in the driveway and I started to jump out and open the door, and then remembered that I couldn't leave the gun in the car with Erin. Things were really going so well that I kept forgetting that there was a plan and I needed to be on top of my game. I couldn't keep slipping up.

I reached back in the car and grabbed the gun. Then, just to lighten the mood, I decided to let Erin in on the punch line.

"Look honey. You're not going to believe this," I said as I opened the cylinder and spun it.

"I forgot to load the gun. I realized it while you were putting zip-ties on Luke. Isn't that kinda funny?"

I immediately knew that I shouldn't have strayed from the plan. Erin looked furious and started yanking on the door handle.

Fortunately, the child locks were still on. I was starting to panic because if she got out of that car and started screaming or running, my plan would be ruined. I needed the time with her inside to convince her that this was the right course for us.

I sprinted to the garage and entered the code. As the garage door opened, I ran back to the car. Erin was trying to climb over the console and reach the child lock button on the door that I had left open. I jumped back in and shut the door, shoving Erin back into her seat.

"Erin, I don't need a gun to be stronger than you. Now you've been cooperative the whole way here. Why are you acting up now? I'm not going to hurt you."

She threw a punch and hit me square in the mouth. She split my lip and blood started to trickle onto my yellow shirt. I'd had enough blood for one day! I shoved her head with the palm of my hand as I drove into the garage and parked next to my Camry. I jumped out of the car with the gun and duffel bag. I was walking toward the garage door button to close the door while trying to load the revolver. Erin was climbing over the consol and into the driver seat and exiting the car as the garage door closed behind us and I pointed the gun at her.

"Really Rob, you brought me all the way back here to shoot me? How does that accomplish your plan? Go ahead. Go ahead and shoot me."

"Erin, I really don't want to shoot you, but I can promise you; I've waited eight long years to be with you and I'm not going to lose you again. You've given yourself to every meathead and douche-bag that smiled in your direction while I've sat idly by and been the perfect gentleman, vying for your attention. No more Mr. Nice Guy!

"Tell me Erin, what did Steve have that I don't have? How about Randy? Luke? What do any of those guys have that you couldn't have with me? I'm the one who's loved you. I'm the one who has sacrificed and dedicated the last eight years of my life to you.

"Why do they get to enjoy your conversations? Your time? Your body?"

"Is that it Rob? Is that what this is about? You've had plenty of conversations with me, probably more than anyone else. You've had time with me, at least as much as anyone else. Is this about my body? Is that what this is about Rob? The fact that I've been in love with and slept with other men, but not you? What are you going to do? Are you going to rape me now?"

"Erin, it isn't rape when love is involved. I have been dreaming about you and your body and being with you since I was 15 years old. But I respected you. I respected what your father preached in Sunday school. I've saved myself for you."

"Rob, lots of guys dream about girl's bodies when they're teenagers. Hell, lots of times they have wet dreams about girl's bodies. But most guys don't force the girl they claim to love at gun point to have sex."

"Erin, I hope you know that I would never hurt you."

"You keep saying that Rob, but since the sun came up today all you have done is hurt me. If you attempt to have sex with me, it will not be consensual under any circumstances. But if that's what we have to do for you to let me go, then let's have at it."

"What do you mean?"

"What I mean is, let's screw. That's what you want isn't it? Will you let me leave and return to my boyfriend if you get a chance to screw me?"

"Erin, that's not how I want it to be. I've been thinking about this for years. I always wanted to wait until our wedding night. It would be the most passionate night of our lives."

Erin took her tank top off over her head and started unbuttoning her shorts.

"What are you doing Erin?"

"We're going to do this Rob. Right here in the garage. Do you want me to bend over the hood of the Beemer? Will that make you really feel like a man?"

"Erin, no! We're not doing anything in the garage. Pick up your clothes and go inside."

"And if I don't? What? You'll shoot me?"

"Erin, I really think we need to go inside and talk this out. I don't want our first time together to be under these conditions."

"You're pathetic Rob. You have a nearly naked woman standing in front of you, offering herself to you and you have no clue what to do. You want to go inside and talk about it?"

"Erin, go in the goddamned house!" I screamed as I grabbed her arm and lead her inside. I was mostly dragging her, in her bra and panties, through the laundry room and down the hallway. Inside the bedroom I tossed her on the bed.

"Oh yeah, this is so much more romantic Rob! This is going to be the most passionate moment of our lives. I bet it will be so amazing that I'll fall head over heels in love with you and call Luke and tell him I'm never coming home. Is that all part of the plan Rob? Once I make love to you I'll never want another? Ohh, I can't wait."

At this particular moment, I couldn't stand the sound of her voice. I needed time to think about what my next move would be and I needed a drink. I took the zip-ties from the duffel bag and put one around each wrist and each ankle.

"Wow, I've heard about stuff like this, but I've never been with a man adventurous enough to try it. I hope you have some toys too. I've never really used those either."

I used another zip-tie to connect her wrists together and one for her ankles. I used one final zip-tie to connect everything. Erin was hog-tied on my bed.

"Okay Rob, I'm ready. Show me what you're made of," she mocked.

I reached back in the duffel bag and got the Duct tape. All I could think about was not hearing the sound of her voice and drinking a scotch or six.

I placed the tape over her mouth and she started to calm down, although I couldn't quite place the look in her eyes. It was somewhere between terrified and pissed off, with a little passion thrown in. I opted to recognize the passion. I brushed her hair out of her face and gently kissed her on the forehead.

Less than 12 hours ago she had looked so beautiful and peaceful in this same exact bed. Less than 12 hours ago we were moments away from sharing sweet, passionate love in this same exact bed. Now, she looked horrible and the sound of her voice was making me ill. I really needed a drink.

"Erin, sweetheart, I'm going to give you a few minutes to calm down. I promise I'll be right back and we'll talk about this. Think very carefully about what you want to say when I take the tape off your mouth."

It was very mumbled, with the tape and all, but it sounded kind of like she said "Skrrru ewe Ob!"

I went to the basement and poured a scotch.

Ladue

XL

Kristy walked down the basement stairs in her house.

"Hey Brad. Did you know that Rob and Erin are back?"

"No, did they return the car?"

"No, I was out front watering the flowers when they pulled in the driveway. It looked like they were fighting. Rob put the car in his garage and closed the door. I wasn't trying to eavesdrop, but I could hear them yelling in the garage. Brad, I think maybe you should go over there and see if everything is okay."

"I don't know honey. I don't know if we should get involved in their argument."

"You didn't see it Brad. This wasn't just some lover's quarrel. This looked bad. And why did he put your car in his garage?"

"I don't know. I guess maybe I could go over and knock on the door and see if everything is okay."

XLI

I took a sip of scotch. I had nearly forgotten about Erin busting my lip, but the burn of the scotch quickly reminded me. One or two of these and I wouldn't be feeling it any more. If I was going to go back upstairs and deal with her I would probably need five or six.

About the time I was finishing my second, I heard the knock at the door. Crap! I bet it's Brad wanting his car back. Didn't he tell me I could use it? He didn't put a time frame on how long I could use it. How did he even know we were back? Maybe it wasn't Brad. Maybe it was the pool guy and I could just tell him to go on around back and take care of the pool.

I went upstairs and opened the front door. Sure enough it was Brad.

"Hey buddy. I saw you pull in the driveway a little while ago and put the car in the garage. I don't need it back or anything, I just wanted to make sure everything went well on your drive."

"Oh yeah. It was great. Thank you so much for letting us borrow it. We bought a few groceries while we were out and I pulled in the garage to unload the car. I hit the door button without even thinking about it and the door closed behind me. Erin's taking a bath and I just finished putting groceries away and I was getting ready to bring it back over to you."

"Not a problem. Looks like you got a pretty nasty gash on your lip. It kinda matches the one on your head and eye."

146

"Yeah. Tell me about it. Trying to navigate to the bathroom in a new house in the middle of the night is one thing, but trying to get out of an unfamiliar car, with low seats, while continuing a conversation with the passenger; I guess results in nearly eating the door frame. It looks worse than it really is."

"I hope so. You're going to have one heck of a story for your first day of work tomorrow."

"Yep. That thought has already crossed my mind. Maybe they'll give me a few days before they take the picture for my badge."

"Oh, I hadn't even thought about that."

Erin was doing her best to scream through the tape. I could hear her muffled screams, but Brad was outside the door and didn't seem to notice. Maybe the neighbor's lawnmower was drowning out the sound. In any event, I needed to get rid of him, now!

"Hey, do you want me to give you the keys so you can take your car home, or, I can bring it over in about an hour. Erin's just getting out of the tub, if you know what I mean?"

"I know exactly what you mean buddy. I really don't need the car back, but just to save you from having to get out later, why don't I just go ahead and take it now. That way, just in case your hour turns in to two or three, you won't have to worry about it, if you know what I mean?"

"Yep. Go around to the garage and I'll open it up and toss you the keys. And thanks again Brad. We had a great time cruising the city in it."

"No problem. Any time."

XLII

I opened the garage door and saw Brad standing in the driveway. Erin was really making a lot of noise now so I stepped out into the garage and closed the door to the laundry room behind me. I tossed Brad the keys and thanked him again.

"Like I said Rob, any time."

Brad backed the car out of the garage and I waved to him as I went back in the door to the laundry room and pushed the garage button on my way in. Brad was backing out of the driveway as the door closed and I went back to the basement to pour another scotch before I went back upstairs to try and talk some sense into Erin.

XLIII

Brad pulled the car into his garage and Kristy came out from the kitchen to meet him.

"You're right Kristy. There's something going on in that house that isn't right. Erin's car isn't there, but Rob said she was in the bathtub. He has a nasty gash on his lip. The clothes that Erin was wearing last night were on the garage floor and I could hear something from inside the house while I was standing at the front door. It could have been music from another room or possibly a dishwasher or washing machine, but Rob seemed nervous and in a hurry to get me out of there.

"I'm going to walk back over next door and see if I can figure out what's going on."

"Brad, why don't we just call the police? You were the one who didn't want to get involved."

"I'm just going to investigate a little bit and make sure everything's okay. I don't think we should call the police on our neighbors when we don't even know that there's something wrong."

"You just said that something isn't right over there."

"I know, but I don't know what it is yet. Let me go look around a little before we jump to conclusions."

XLIV

I slammed two more drinks and poured another before I headed back up the stairs. It was time to focus again on the plan. It was time to think again about the words that I was going to use to win Erin back. We needed to be able to sit and have a real conversation without her being defensive and antagonizing me. I wanted to take the tape off her mouth, cut the zip-ties, have her put some clothes on and go sit by the pool and talk to me. It remained to be seen whether or not that was going to be an option.

I walked into the bedroom and she started thrashing about on the bed. She was trying to yell at me through her taped mouth. I sat on the edge of the bed.

"Erin, sweetheart. This wasn't part of my plan. I hate seeing you like this. I want to be able to have a real conversation with you. Do you think if I remove the tape and the zip-ties that maybe we can go outside and talk?"

She nodded her head in agreement.

I slowly removed the tape and she gasped as if she had just come up from under water. I grabbed the duffel bag to get a knife and cut the zip-ties.

"Rob," I heard her say behind me.

"You may as well kill me now. You are completely delusional and psychotic and schizophrenic if you think that we are ever going to have a normal relationship. I offered myself to you if you would let me go, but that wasn't enough for you. I'm convinced that you are never going to let me go. And if that's the case, then please, just kill me now."

"Erin, sweetie, I'm not going to kill you. I've never even thought about killing you. But, you're right; I'm also never going to let you go. We were so close to perfection last night and then I blew it. I'll never let that happen again. I'll never lose you again like I did this morning. I was so afraid that you were gone for good and I might never get another chance with you.

"But I did. I did get another chance and it's meant to be. Don't you see Erin; we've always been meant to be together. And I don't want just your body. At least not in the way that you think I do. I want to become one with your body. I want us to be together forever, either in this life or the next."

"Rob, we're not going to the same place in the next life, so if that's where I need to go to get away from you, then please, let's just get it over with."

I considered what she was saying. Although she hadn't been as pure as I always imagined, I also didn't think she was going to hell. Maybe this would be our only way to spend eternity together. Kind of like Romeo and Juliet. I imagined in my mind that we would make sweet love and then together, we would end our time on this earth, rising to the heavens to spend eternity with the angels. It certainly wasn't part of the plan, but maybe it was better.

XLV

Brad had circled the house and found nothing out of place on the exterior. He came back around to the front of the house and thought about knocking again on the front door, but decided that instead he would just try the doorknob. It was unlocked.

He slowly opened the front door and walked in, trying to think of a good reason why he was in the house should everything turn out to be fine. Maybe Erin and Rob were together in the bedroom like any normal couple would be and he could slowly creep in, assess the situation and slowly creep out. In Brad's mind, that would be ideal.

Brad was wearing flip-flops and he kicked them off at the front door, hoping to make less noise. He walked straight toward the hallway that lead to the bedroom. He was halfway down the hallway when he heard Erin say, "I'm convinced that you are never going to let me go. And if that's the case, then please, just kill me now."

The door to the bedroom was mostly closed, but Brad could see the back of Rob and see Erin hog-tied on the bed. He could see that Rob held a knife in his hand. Brad's heart was beating so loud that he could hear and feel his pulse in his ears. He was afraid that if he left to go call the police, one or both of them would be dead by the time the police arrived.

He heard Erin say, "Then please, let's just get it over with." And then there was silence. Brad's mind was racing as quickly as his heart. What in the world could be going through Rob's mind? Certainly he wasn't thinking about killing the love of his life, was he? But, murder-suicide that might be something that Rob would entertain.

Brad knew that Rob had a weapon, and he had nothing but his fists. What if Rob had more than a knife? What if he had a gun in his waistband? Brad wondered if he could get to Rob fast enough to disarm him before he could hurt Erin?

Brad was weighing his options when he heard Rob say, "Erin, I've never wanted to hurt you. I can't bear the thought of causing you pain. All I've ever wanted is for you to love me as much as I love you. If the only place that our love can be mutual is in the afterlife, then I'm ready to go there. Please understand that this isn't what I wanted for us." Rob was crying now.

"We're never going to see the grandkids in the backyard, you know that don't you? But, if this is the only way, then it's the only way. I love you dear. More than you will ever know. I promise, I'll see you on the other side."

Those were Rob Anderson's last words.

XLVI

It became apparent to me that there was only one way that this could end. There was no point continuing my life without Erin. And, really she was right. Even if we spent the evening together that I had imagined and she fell in love with me and called Luke to tell him that she wasn't coming home, he was still going to be kinda pissed about the whole ordeal.

He would probably press charges and since he's an attorney, he would have attorney buddies who made sure that I got the maximum sentence. I don't know how much that would be, but after today, any time away from Erin would be unbearable.

What would she do during my time in jail? I would certainly get more than probation. A couple months? A year? The longest I had gone without talking to Erin since the day we met was the two weeks that my family went on vacation in Louisiana and neither of us had a cell phone. Since I returned from that trip, there wasn't a single time that 48 hours had passed without a phone call, a text, an email or a face-to-face conversation.

Assuming that I could make her fall in love with me during the next 12 hours, which I really think I could, then what? I'm pretty sure that I couldn't survive prison. I couldn't survive knowing that I had taken every risk and finally won her over and then I was going to go away. Sure, it might be worth it to make sweet love as the sun comes up in the morning, with a woman who is truly as in love with me as I am with her. But, it was only a matter of time until the knock at the door and then I would be lead away in handcuffs to an uncertain future.

The only future that was certain right now was that if we both died right here, we would be together forever in the afterlife. I couldn't bear the thought of being away from her again.

"Erin, I've never wanted to hurt you. I can't bear the thought of causing you pain. All I've ever wanted is for you to love me as much as I love you. If the only place that our love can be mutual is in the afterlife, then I'm ready to go there. Please understand that this isn't what I wanted for us." I was crying now. I couldn't help it. The tears and sobs were coming bigger and stronger with every attempt to breathe.

"We're never going to see the grandkids in the backyard, you know that don't you? But, if this is the only way, then it's the only way. I love you dear. More than you will ever know. I promise: I'll see you on the other side."

I still wondered if we could make love before the end of our time on earth. I figured the only way to find out was to cut her zip-ties and see if she tried to fight me, or if she embraced me. I stepped toward her with the knife to cut her loose.

I felt a sharp blow to the back of my head. It was right at the base of my neck. I saw spots in front of my eyes and couldn't take a deep breath. I didn't want to, but I was falling forward onto the bed. My shoulders and arms were numb and I felt a twitching in my back muscles. Erin was still tied, and I was afraid that I would land on her when I hit the bed, knife still in my hand.

Although my arms were numb from the blow by Brad, I did my best to turn my body so that I wouldn't land on her. I landed hard on the bed and the blade. It went into my neck right above my collarbone. The cold metal actually burned an intense heat.

Maybe it had missed everything important. Although at that moment I really didn't care. I couldn't speak, but I could see. Erin was lying across from me, just like last night. Only now she was lying toward me. Our bodies once again shared a bed, this time more passionate than the last.

Our eyes met. She still had the most beautiful face I had ever seen. I'm pretty sure that making sweet love was out of the question, because I began spitting up blood. My second big, sputtering cough resulted in tiny splatters all over her face. I thought I saw sorrow in her eyes. If she could feel sorrow for me, possibly she could feel love.

Passing away before Erin was always part of my plan, of course I imagined we would be in our late eighties or early nineties. I always thought I would die peacefully in my sleep. Maybe sit down in the recliner for a late afternoon nap and never wake up.

Uncle Rich had said something one time about life being full of surprises, some good and some bad, but that's what makes life so enjoyable. Uncle Rich was usually a jokester and he wasn't very good at the philosophical stuff, but maybe he was onto something.

However, he also said that over-planning is like reading the last chapter of a book first; it takes all the mystery and excitement out of life. All along, the last chapter of my book included me passing away before Erin and then the two of us spending eternity together in the afterlife. And here we are; my last chapter playing out just as I planned it. Yep, I was right; Uncle Rich never was very good at the philosophical stuff.

I took one last, labored, deep breath, knowing that life on this earth was slipping from me. As I faded out, I looked deep in her eyes and mouthed the words, "I love you."

I'm not for certain, but I think I might have blinked a few more times before I was finally gone. It was during one of those blinks that I know I saw her mouth the words back to me.

EPILOUGE

My relationship with Luke never really recovered. We tried to reconcile and then we tried to go on like nothing happened; and then we tried couples therapy. I think Luke recovered, but I never did.

I tried quitting school and moving back home. That was a horrible idea. Everything I saw everyday was a reminder of Rob. Trying to lay low in Shelbyville wasn't going to work.

I went back to school and finished my law degree. I thought that being an activist for battered and abused women would help heal me. I was wrong. I empathized with my clients, but I couldn't bear to hear the details of their abuse over and over, day in and day out.

Although I knew my torment was over, I couldn't erase it. A man was dead, and I was forever connected to his death. Each night as I lay awake I replay years of interaction in my mind. Had I done something to lead him on? Had I been a willing participant in the world he created in his mind? I guess I really always knew that Rob Anderson loved me, and in some ways, it was a comfort that I took for granted.

Night after night I lay awake and hate him for what he has done to my life. I curse him through my tears for his ability to reduce me to a shell of my former self. He was the narcissist! He was the social outcast! He was weak and a coward! How can I continue to allow thoughts of him to control my life? He has achieved in death what he was unable to do in life; he is forever on my mind.

And then, there are those nights when I try to tell myself that the only way to move forward from this is to forgive. Out loud I tell myself, "I forgive Rob Anderson for what he did to me. Heavenly Father, please take pity on his soul."

And occasionally, for reasons that I don't understand and I can never speak about to anyone else, I find myself wondering, "What would life with Rob Anderson have been like?"

Maybe I'm really becoming delusional or sleep deprivation is driving me insane, but that is one of the questions I ask myself in the wee morning hours when sleep escapes me. He certainly loved me, more than any other man I have ever known.

And then, just before daybreak; just before I have to drag myself from the comfort of my bed and another sleepless night and somehow face the day, I wonder; what is love? What does it really feel like? What does it really look like? How will I ever know if I really find it?

And I am reminded; Rob Anderson never had to ask himself those questions. He knew. He knew who he was in love with and there was no doubt in his mind. As many problems as Rob had; as much as he was removed from reality; Rob knew that he was in love with me; and he would be until the day he died.

And this is what haunts me.

ABOUT THE AUTHOR

Neal R. Minor has always enjoyed writing, but for most of his life, life has gotten in the way of writing anything more than a short story that gets tossed in a dark drawer or saved in a never-to-be-seen-again file on the computer.

When Neal turned 40 he decided that it was time to make time and actually write a book. Ladue is the first of what he hopes will be many more titles.

Neal lives in Monroe City, MO where he runs an insurance business and is the town Mayor. In addition to writing, Neal likes to spend time with his fiancée Melissa, taking care of their chickens and trying to keep up with the activities that their six children are involved in.

www.ingramcontent.com/pod-product-compliance
Lightning Source LLC
Chambersburg PA
CBHW070329130626
46556CB00007B/2778